Clint Slater

McCOY'S LAST RIDE

McCoy's Last Bet

First published in eBook and paperback 2025

Contents

CHAPTER 2: A DEAL IN THE DARK 19

CHAPTER 3: BLOOD ON THE BADGE 31

CHAPTER 4: RIDING FOR THE LAW 43

CHAPTER 5: A JUST CAUSE 56

CHAPTER 6: THE HUNT FOR JED ROYCE 66

CHAPTER 7: THE ILLUSION OF JUSTICE 76

CHAPTER 8: CRACKS IN THE LAW 87

CHAPTER 7: A BAD FEELING GETS WORSE 96

CHAPTER 8: THE COST OF PROTECTION 103

CHAPTER 9: THE LAW AIN'T COMING 120

CHAPTER 10: A DANGEROUS PROPOSITION 130

CHAPTER 11: THE SET-UP 143

CHAPTER 12: THE TRAP IS SPRUNG 148

CHAPTER 13: THE LAST STAND 154

CHAPTER 14: MCKINNRICK'S FALL 163

CHAPTER 15: BLEEDING AND RUNNING 170

CHAPTER 16: GHOSTS ON HIS TRAIL 178

CHAPTER 17: NO PLACE LEFT TO RUN 185

EPILOGUE: A MAN CALLED MCCOY 197

INTRODUCTION

The saloon was warm with the scent of whiskey and cigar smoke, the low murmur of voices blending with the occasional clatter of poker chips and the scrape of chairs against the wooden floor. The place was neither fine nor filthy, the kind of establishment that catered to men with money but didn't much care how they got it.

Wesley McCoy sat at a table near the back, his coat draped over the chair, the flickering lamplight glinting off the polished silver buttons on his vest. His hat sat low, casting a shadow across his sharp features, but his eyes never missed a damn thing. He wasn't drunk, but he had a good whiskey glow, just enough to soften the edges of the world.

On the table in front of him sat the last hand of the night, the one that had won him a tidy sum. The other players had grumbled, some laughing, some bitter, but none accusing him of cheating. They knew better.

McCoy let his fingers trail over the edges of his winnings—stacked coins, a few bills, a pocket watch he'd won off a rancher who'd bet foolishly. His mind wasn't on the cards, though.

It was on how he got here.

He swirled the whiskey in his glass, watching the firelight dance in its depths, the sound of his own name echoing in his head—his new name.

Wesley McCoy.

He'd been called something else once, a long damn time ago.

Wes Harlan.

A cattle driver, a drifter, a man who never thought much past his next job. A man who'd walked into a saloon just like this one looking for a good game of cards, a full belly, and a warm bed for the night. That night had changed everything. He took a slow sip of whiskey, letting it burn down deep.

He had been a different man then—thought different, dressed different. A little rough around the edges, but not yet the kind of man who knew how to hide in plain sight. That was before McKinnrick. Before the law turned on him. Before he saw firsthand how fast a man could lose his name, his reputation, his whole damn life.

He reached for the deck of cards, absently shuffling them, the familiar rasp of paper against calloused fingers grounding him.

A man can change when he needs to.

And he had needed to.

The man who had walked into that saloon in Garrison was long gone.

Now, there was just McCoy.

And he wasn't about to let the past catch up with him.

CHAPTER 1: 6 MONTHS AGO

The Silver Spur Saloon was thick with smoke and sweat, the kind of place where men came to drink, gamble, and forget how mean the world was. The air was heavy with the stink of cheap whiskey, unwashed bodies, and the lingering scent of gunpowder—a place where fortunes turned quick and a man's life could be lost over the wrong hand of cards.

Wes Harlan sat at a table near the back, his hat pulled low, the brim casting a shadow over sharp, sun-creased features. A week's worth of dust clung to his coat, and his boots bore the wear of too many miles in the saddle. His lean frame carried the kind of wiry strength that came from years on the trail, the muscle built from swinging a branding iron, drawing a gun, and everything in between.

His hair was dark, worn longer than most, brushing against the collar of his shirt, and his jaw carried the rough beginnings of a beard—just enough to say he hadn't cared to shave, but not enough to mark him as a man who'd let himself go. His eyes, though, were what most men noticed first. A cold, calculating blue, the color of a sky before a hard rain. The kind of eyes that measured a room, a man, a situation—always watching, always weighing the odds.

Harlan was a man used to keeping his back to the wall and his right hand close to his gun. Not because he was looking for trouble, but because trouble had a way of finding him. He wasn't an outlaw, not in the way folks liked to think of one.

McCoy's Last Bet

He'd never strung a man up, never robbed a bank, never taken something that wasn't his. But he wasn't exactly honest either. He took work where it came— cattle drives, ranch hand jobs, and when the trail bosses needed a man who could handle trouble, he was the one they paid extra. Because Harlan was handy with an iron. And that was worth something in the kind of places he drifted through.

Harlan had just been paid off after weeks of hard riding, driving cattle across dry, sun-baked country. The pay wasn't much, but it was enough to make a man feel like he'd earned a night to himself. A game of poker, a belly full of whiskey, and a woman to keep his bed warm—that was the plan. A simple thing. A man's right after weeks of dust and labor.

The oil lamps swung lazy from their chains, throwing flickering light over the faces of the men hunched around the poker table. The shuffle of cards. The scrape of chair legs against rough floorboards. The slow, deliberate clink of silver coins stacking higher with every bet.

Jeb Tolliver sat across from him, a big rancher gone to seed, his gut pressing against his belt, his thick fingers twitching against his cards. Sweat glistened on his forehead, though the night air outside was cool. He smelled like tobacco spit and bad decisions.

To Tolliver's left, Lyle Coates, a wiry gambler with a slick smile that never quite reached his eyes. He chewed on a matchstick, watching the game like a man who already knew where it was going. Next round the table was West Gage. Harlan knew the man, he'd worked a drive for him a few years back, pushing longhorns across the frontier, back when the only trouble they had was river crossings and the occasional rustler. Gage had been the same then as he was now—quiet, steady, a man who let his presence do the talking. He didn't waste words, didn't bother with small talk. The kind of cattle boss who never had to raise his voice to be listened to.

Harlan respected him for that. But respect wouldn't do him much good here. Not with the way Gage was looking at him now, pale eyes flat and unreadable, like he was sizing up a horse at auction, deciding whether it was worth the trouble or better put down. Gage took poker seriously.

The deck moved between them, hands played, whiskey poured. Harlan had been winning steady, but not enough to make enemies—just enough to stay in the game. A few barmaids worked the room, their voices sweet, but their eyes calculating. They smiled, leaned in close, took what coins they could from the men too drunk or too lonely to care. The Silver Spur Saloon was humming, packed tight with ranch hands, drifters, and the kind of men who lived and died between the rim of a whiskey glass and the barrel of a Colt. A few rough-looking cowboys leaned against the bar, shouting over one another, some already spoiling for a fight. A piano clinked somewhere in the back, a tune half-drowned by the noise of the room. Somewhere in the corner, a drunk was slumped over, snoring into his own spilled beer. The place was alive, pulsing with tension just beneath the surface, the way all saloons were in towns like this.

Harlan didn't look up when the next hand was dealt. He could already feel the night turning. Harlan lifted his whiskey glass, tilting it just enough to wet his lips without really drinking. The liquor was cheap and burned in all the wrong ways, but it gave him something to do with his hands. More importantly, it let him watch the men across the table without seeming like he was watching.

At the poker table, the stakes were high. Silver dollars, crumpled bills, and the occasional gold coin sat in uneven stacks in the center. The players were deep in their cups, the whiskey making their hands looser and their nerves tighter.

Jeb Tolliver's mustache was dark with tobacco juice, and every so often, he'd spit into the sawdust beside his boot, his heavy jowls quivering as he chewed on the end of an unlit cigar. Jeb wasn't smart, but he thought he was. That made him dangerous. He wiped his forehead with the back of his thick wrist, glaring at his cards as if sheer willpower might change them. "Boys," he grunted, "I do believe this here is my night."

Beside him, Lyle Coates smirked, the matchstick in his teeth shifting as he chewed on it. Lyle was lean as a snake and twice as slippery, a gambler with the kind of face you wanted to punch on sight. His fingers tapped idly against the table, his eyes flicking from player to player, calculating.

"Every man says that 'til he's walking home broke," Lyle drawled, flashing Harlan a knowing grin.

Harlan said nothing. Just shifted his weight, tilting his hat lower over his eyes. West Gage sat to his right, silent as stone. He barely moved, except to drink, except to play his cards. Watching Harlan closely, trying to work out how good his hand was.

The last man at the table, Blake, was jittery. A drifter, by the look of him—dirty, unshaven, his hands too twitchy for a man used to holding cards. Probably lost more than he won, and from the way his leg bounced under the table, he was losing now.

The next hand was dealt.

Harlan slid his cards toward him, slow. He peeled up the corners, taking a glance. Three kings. A damn fine hand. Not the best, but good enough to hold his own.

He kept his face still, unreadable.

The others studied their own cards, reactions ranging from tight-lipped to outright cocky. Jeb Tolliver let out a grunt, his eyes lighting up like he'd just been handed the deed to half of Arizona. A bad liar with a good hand.

The betting started. Harlan let it play out, let the whiskey do the talking for them. Blake folded immediately, licking his lips like he was sick to his stomach. His fingers twitched toward his empty whiskey glass, but he didn't have the coin for another. Gage pushed a small stack forward, quiet, measured. Lyle hesitated, then matched the bet with a shrug.

Tolliver, already drunk and overconfident, let out a loud chuckle and slammed half of his stack of bills into the pile. "Let's get serious, boys."

Harlan sat back in his chair, rolling his shoulders like a man who wasn't concerned. A long night could be won or lost on the strength of patience alone. The final bets were made.

Tolliver leaned forward, his breath sour. "Well, boys, reckon I'll make this interesting." He shoved what was left of his cash into the pile. "All in."

Lyle whistled low, shaking his head. "Hell, Jeb, thought you were trying to make it home with somethin' in your pockets."

Tolliver grinned, his face red and slick with liquor. He was already picturing himself walking away with it all. Harlan took his time. He didn't like rushing. Didn't like showing too much of himself too fast. He'd been in too many saloons, too many games, too many nights like this to make that mistake. He studied Tolliver's face, that wide, arrogant grin, the glint of sweat rolling down his temple. Drunk, overconfident, already counting the money before the cards hit the wood.

Harlan let a long, slow breath out through his nose. Then he slid his stack of coins forward, matching the bet. "Call."

The men around the table went quiet. The whores by the bar were watching now, their smiles fading, their hands resting light on the shoulders of men too deep in their cups to notice. The bartender stood still, rubbing a dirty rag over the same spot on the counter, waiting.

Tolliver slapped his cards down, his grin wide enough to split his face. Two pair. Aces and eights.

Lyle let out a low whistle. "Damn, Jeb, thought you had somethin' real."

Harlan laid his own cards down, his three kings staring back at them in the lamplight.

For a second, nothing happened.

Then Tolliver's face went red. His grin vanished.

Harlan had seen that look before. The moment a man goes from drunk and cocky to mean and stupid. Tolliver's chair scraped back hard, knocking over a bottle. His voice dropped low, thick with anger. "You son of a bitch."

Harlan didn't move. Didn't blink. He knew where this night was going. And from the way Lyle Coates leaned back, grinning, it was exactly where he wanted it to go.

For a long moment, nothing moved.

Jeb Tolliver's grin was gone, his ruddy face twisted into something darker, something ugly and mean. He stared at the cards like they might rearrange themselves if he looked hard enough. But they didn't.

The three kings sat there in the flickering lamplight, staring back at him, telling him what he already knew—he'd lost. His thick fingers curled against the table, knuckles going white. Then his fist came down hard, rattling the bottles, knocking over a half-empty whiskey glass that splashed into the pot of silver and paper bills. The sound cracked through the saloon like a gunshot.

"You cheated, you son of a bitch!" Tolliver's voice was thick with booze, but there was something else in it now—rage, bruised pride, the kind of anger that only came from a man who couldn't afford to lose.

The room went still.

At the bar, a couple of cowhands stopped their conversation mid-sentence. Men turned from their drinks, their hands drifting toward their guns, slow and natural-like. Not drawing, not yet, but ready. The bartender didn't move. He'd seen nights like this before. Even the whores along the balcony had gone quiet, watching from above with sharp, knowing eyes.

Harlan sat there, still as stone, his fingers resting easy against the worn wood of the table. He didn't lift his whiskey glass. Didn't blink. "You lost fair, Tolliver," Harlan said, his voice calm, even. "Walk away."

Tolliver wasn't hearing it. His hand twitched toward his hip. The shift in the air was immediate, sharp as a knife. From the corner of his eye, Harlan saw Lyle Coates lean back in his chair, his matchstick rolling from one side of his mouth to the other. He wasn't in this, wasn't picking a side—he was just waiting to see if the night turned bloody.

Across the table, West Gage sat quiet, his fingers tapping slow against the wood, his pale eyes fixed on Harlan. He wasn't reaching for his gun, but he wasn't looking away either. Like he was memorizing how this was gonna play out.

Tolliver shoved himself to his feet, his chair scraping loud across the floor, tipping sideways as it knocked over a whiskey bottle. The bottle shattered, the smell of liquor sharp in the air. His fingers curled around the butt of his revolver.

Harlan didn't think. He just moved.

Before Tolliver's iron even cleared leather, Harlan's Colt was already in his hand, already leveled, already firing. The crack of the gunshot slammed through the room. Tolliver jerked backward, his eyes wide, confused, like he didn't understand what had just happened. Like he wasn't sure why his legs weren't working anymore.

He staggered once.

Twice.

Then collapsed hard into a table, sending cards and empty glasses flying as he hit the ground with a heavy, breathless grunt. His hat rolled away. His boots kicked weakly at the floorboards. Then nothing. The whole saloon stood frozen. The air was thick with the sharp bite of gunpowder, the heavy silence of men waiting to see who would move next.

Harlan let out a slow breath, his gun still raised, the hammer still cocked. Tolliver wasn't getting back up.

From the other side of the table, Lyle let out a low whistle. "Well, hell," he said, dragging the matchstick from his lips. "Didn't even give the man a chance."

Harlan didn't answer.

West Gage was still watching him, his fingers no longer tapping, his face unreadable.

Then—

A chair scraped. A man moved.

The drifter, Blake.

Harlan caught the shift just in time—Blake's hand going for his revolver, his eyes wild, desperate. Blake, the jittery drifter, panicked. His fingers twitched, yanked his gun free. The barrel wobbled as he pulled the trigger, his aim wild and desperate. The shot cracked through the saloon. The bullet missed Harlan. But it didn't miss the poor bastard standing at the bar.

A ranch hand in a sweat-stained shirt jerked forward, a red mist blooming from his shoulder. He spun, knocking over a bottle of rye, his knees buckling as he collapsed against the counter. For a heartbeat, the only sound was the whistle of the bullet's echo. Then Harlan turned and fired. His Colt roared, and Blake went stiff—like someone had just yanked his spine out from under him. The bullet punched clean through his ribs, sending him staggering back. His arms flailed, knocking over a chair, his gun clattering useless to the floor.

He hit the ground hard, sucking for air like a fish on dry land. And then the saloon exploded into chaos. Men scrambled from their chairs, sending poker chips and silver dollars clattering to the floor. Bottles shattered, boots stomped, curses flew. Someone overturned a table—a loud crash against the floorboards.

The whores screamed and scattered up the stairs, disappearing into the safety of their rooms. A cowboy near the bar tripped over a spittoon, hit the ground hard, scrambling for cover. Harlan kept his gun raised, turning slow, his breath steady, keeping his back to the wall.

Then the batwing doors slammed open. Eli Grady stepped in, shotgun raised. The sheriff was a big, heavy-set man, built like a ranch mule and just as stubborn. His coat stretched tight over broad shoulders, the iron star pinned on his chest dull with age. His gray mustache twitched as he scanned the room, eyes as cold and unreadable as river stones. He didn't look surprised by the dead men on the floor. Just annoyed.

The barrels of his shotgun swung slow, stopping on Harlan. "Drop it."

Harlan didn't move, his grip still firm around his Colt. "They drew first."

Then Lyle spoke. "I'm not sure that's true, Sherrif. Didn't seem that way to me."

Grady's face didn't change. He shifted his weight, spat into the sawdust, then cocked his head toward the bodies.

"Maybe." His voice was dry as the desert. "But they ain't the ones still breathin'."

A movement behind Grady—two deputies stepping in, revolvers drawn. Well. That settled that. Harlan exhaled through his nose, thumbed back the hammer, then slowly let it down. He lowered the gun, but he didn't let go just yet.

Grady took a step closer, shotgun still leveled. "Ain't tellin' you twice, son."

Harlan's jaw tightened. He let the Colt slip from his fingers. It hit the floorboards with a heavy thud. The deputies moved fast—one yanked Harlan forward, the other grabbed his gun belt. Then the fist came. A sharp crack across Harlan's jaw. His head snapped sideways, blood filling his mouth. He staggered but kept his feet under him. Didn't give them the satisfaction of seeing him fall.

"You boys enjoyin' yourselves?" he muttered, licking blood from his teeth.

The deputy who'd hit him—a weasel-faced bastard with a missing tooth—smirked. "Always nice to keep the gallows warm."

Grady just shook his head, then tipped his shotgun toward the door. "Haul him out."

The deputies dragged Harlan toward the entrance, their grips iron-hard around his arms. The saloon was still quiet, men watching, no one daring to speak.

And then—Lyle Coates. He was still at the table, still leaning back, his slick grin untouched by the mess of bodies and broken glass. He chewed the matchstick slow, tipped his hat as Harlan passed. "Bad luck, Harlan."

McCoy's Last Bet

The deputies shoved him forward, boots scraping over wooden planks, then down into the street. The night air hit him like a slap, crisp and cool against his burning jaw. Then he saw it. The gallows. The noose swayed slightly in the night breeze, the thick rope rough and waiting.

Grady stepped out behind him. "Sunrise," he said, voice matter-of-fact. "Better say your prayers."

The jail cell wasn't much to look at. Stone walls, rough-hewn and damp. A single barred window, too small for a man to fit through. Harlan sat on the cot, hands resting on his thighs, blood pooling in his mouth where the deputy's fist had split his lip. He let his head rest back against the wall. The wood creaked, old and worn. Outside, he could hear the distant sound of boots on the boardwalk, drunken voices slurring their way home, the occasional neigh of a restless horse.

Tomorrow.

Sunrise.

He stared at the ceiling, his breath steady. Unless something changed, he was hanging.

CHAPTER 2: A DEAL IN THE DARK

The cell stank of old sweat, piss, and the slow rot of men who'd spent too long in a place like this. Harlan sat on the rough wooden cot, elbows resting on his knees, staring at nothing in particular. The iron bars cast long shadows across the stone floor in the dim lantern light filtering through the corridor, flickering as if the flame itself was trying to hold its breath.

He ran his tongue over the split in his lip, feeling the raw sting where the deputy's fist had landed. The dull ache in his jaw was nothing compared to the heavier weight sitting in his gut.

This wasn't how the night was supposed to go.

He'd been riding with the drives, pushing cattle across the frontier, working hard under a sun that didn't give a damn whether a man lived or died beneath it. The pay wasn't much, but it was enough, and he knew his way around a herd. More than that, he knew his way around a fight.

And that's why the trail bosses liked him.

Didn't talk much, didn't stir trouble. But when trouble found them, Harlan could end it fast.

It put a few extra dollars in his pocket. Men liked knowing there was someone in the outfit who could handle himself. A hand who wasn't just good with a rope, but with a gun.

The kind of man who didn't have to raise his voice to be heard.

The kind of man who was good to have at your side—but dangerous to have against you.

That's why, when the drive was done, when the cattle had been sold and the money had changed hands, Harlan had a little more in his pocket than some of the others. A few extra silver coins from a boss who appreciated the nights he'd spent keeping men alive and keeping rustlers off their trail. And after two months of dust, bad coffee, and cold camps, he figured he'd earned himself a night.

Just one.

A card game. A belly full of good whiskey. A warm bed and a woman to keep it that way. That was the plan. Instead, he was sitting in a cell, bleeding into his shirt, staring down a noose waiting for sunrise.

Harlan let out a slow breath.

He should've known better. He always knew better. You don't get comfortable at a table full of men who think luck owes them something. You don't let a drunk fool himself into thinking you took what was his. And you sure as hell don't win too much in a place where some men value pride more than their own damn lives.

He could still hear Tolliver's voice in his head, slurred and angry. "You cheated, you son of a bitch!"

The sound of the chair scraping back, the heavy crash of a whiskey bottle hitting the floor. Harlan had known what was coming before Tolliver's hand ever went to his hip. That's why Harlan was still breathing, and Tolliver wasn't. And that's why he was here, sitting in the dark, waiting for morning.

One bad hand. One wrong bet.

And now, his luck was running out.

Harlan sat on the splintered cot, elbows on his knees, head tilted back against the cold stone wall. The bruise on his jaw throbbed, the dull ache settling deep into his bones, but he ignored it. The real hurt wasn't the kind that could be rubbed out.

It was the gallows waiting outside.

The jailhouse was silent, save for the occasional drip of water somewhere in the dark. The sheriff and his deputies had long since retired, leaving Harlan alone with nothing but his thoughts and the distant sounds of Garrison sleeping.

He could hear it—the town breathing in the night.

The jail felt like a tomb, the air thick and stale, pressed in by the weight of old sweat and bad decisions. He could still taste the copper of his own blood, where the deputy's fist had split his lip. His jaw ached, the kind of deep, lingering pain that would sit with him for a few days, if he made it that long.

But that wasn't the real problem.

The real problem was outside.

Beyond these walls, beyond the locked door and the sleeping deputies, a noose swayed in the night breeze, waiting for the sun to rise. That old rope, that empty space beneath it.

Waiting for him.

His breath came slow and steady, though his heart worked against it, beating a little too hard, a little too fast. He wasn't afraid of dying. Not in the way most men were. He'd seen too much death, carried it in his hands, left it in his wake.

But hanging?

That was different.

Harlan had watched a man die that way once, back in Abilene. Rope too short. The bastard had choked on his own tongue for near ten minutes, kicking like a gored bull before the life finally drained out of him. And that's if the hangman knew his business. If he didn't, a man could dangle there half an hour, fighting for air, clawing at nothing.

No, Harlan didn't like the idea of dying that way.

So he took stock of his options.

Try to Break Out. Not likely.

The cell was solid stone and iron, built for drunks, thieves, and men waiting to swing. The deputies weren't smart, but they were mean, and mean men slept light. Even if he managed to get past them, even if he made it out the door, where the hell would he go?

Sheriff Grady wasn't the kind of lawman to let things slide. If Harlan bolted, the whole damn town would be on his heels before he even got to his horse—if he still had a horse.

So that was out.

Option Two: Sit Here and Let the Rope Do Its Work.

Even less appealing. Harlan exhaled slow, rolling his shoulders against the ache settling deep in his bones. He didn't kid himself—he wasn't a good man. He wasn't innocent. He'd killed plenty of men, some deserving, some maybe not. But he sure as hell wasn't going to sit here and make it easy for them.

Which left…

Option Three: Wait and See.

Maybe dumb luck would come his way. He'd never been much for prayers, but luck and trouble had always followed him close, and right now, he needed one more than the other. He shifted, glancing toward the door, the dim glow of the lantern in the hallway stretching long across the floor. Somewhere in the dark, a dog barked. Somewhere further, a horse snorted, restless. And then—boots on the boardwalk. Harlan lifted his head, his shoulders going tight. Not a drunk. Not some cowboy stumbling home. A man with a purpose.

The footsteps came slowly on the wooden floor. Not the hurried shuffle of a deputy coming to check on his prisoner, not the lazy drag of a drunk being hauled in for the night. No—this was something else. This was a man who wasn't in a hurry, but knew the world would move for him anyway.

Harlan lifted his head slightly from where he sat on the cot, his back still pressed against the damp stone wall. He didn't straighten all the way, didn't give the impression he was too interested. But he was listening. Boots on wood. Even, deliberate. Whoever was coming wasn't just passing through.

The steps reached the doorway. The figure stepped into view, blocking the light from the hallway lantern. Even in the dim glow, Harlan could see the kind of man he was looking at. Tall and broad across the shoulders, built thick like a man who'd spent years in the saddle, years carrying the weight of something heavy. His face was lined and weathered, his skin darkened from too many long days beneath a cruel sun.

He wasn't young, but he wasn't old either—he carried himself like a man still in his prime, though the edges had been worn down by hard miles and harder choices.

His coat was worn but clean, hanging open just enough to show the iron strapped to his waist.

His gun belt sat low on his hips, the revolver tied down like it had been that way for years. Not the kind of man who was quick to draw. The kind who didn't need to be.

His boots were polished but well-worn. A scar cut across his left cheek, thin but deep, old enough that it had settled into the rest of his rough-hewn features, like it belonged there. And his eyes—cold, knowing, the color of gunmetal just before it turns hot.

Harlan had seen that look before. It wasn't the look of a sheriff. It wasn't the look of an outlaw either. It was something in between.

The newcomer stopped just outside the cell, resting one hand lightly on the bars. He didn't grip them, didn't shake them like a man impatient. He just stood there, watching. Then—the smallest of smirks. "You don't look like a man ready to die."

His voice was low, easy, but there was a weight to it, like every word had been considered before it left his mouth. Harlan exhaled slow. He hadn't expected company, but that didn't mean he was in a rush to entertain it.

"Ain't got much say in it."

The man let out a quiet chuckle, tilting his head slightly. "That so?"

He stepped back, grabbed a chair that had been sitting against the opposite wall, and pulled it forward in an unhurried motion, the legs scraping against the wood. He turned it backward before settling into it, his arms resting easy across the top, one boot stretched out, the other planted firm. Took his time. Like he wasn't in a jailhouse at all. Like he was just passing the time with an old friend. For a moment, he said nothing. Just let the silence hang between them, like the noose waiting outside. Then, finally—"Names McKinnrick. And I know your name."

Harlan didn't react. Didn't flinch.

McKinnrick watched him, that faint smirk still playing at his lips, though his eyes stayed cold. "Seen you in a few places, heard a few stories." He nodded once, like he was settling on a thought. "You ain't some cheap cattle thief, so I got to wonder—how's a man like you end up about to swing in a town like this?"

Harlan rolled his shoulders, his back still against the wall. He wasn't in the mood for a history lesson. "Bad hand of cards. Bad luck."

McKinnrick let out another quiet chuckle. Not mocking. Just amused. "Son, we all got bad luck." He leaned in just a fraction, his voice dropping. "Difference is, some of us know how to make it work for us."

His meaning sat heavy in the air between them. Harlan just watched him, waiting. Whatever this was, it wasn't just a conversation for the sake of passing time. McKinnrick was here for a reason. McKinnrick sat easy in the chair, like he had all the time in the world, like he wasn't sitting in a jailhouse talking to a condemned man. The lantern glow caught the edges of his features—sharp cheekbones, weathered skin, the deep lines of a man who'd spent too many years in the saddle and too many nights under the stars. He let the silence settle between them, comfortable in it, before he finally leaned forward, resting both arms on the chair's back.

His voice dipped lower, quieter now, but it lost none of its weight. "I got men. I got work. And I got a problem that needs solving." He tilted his head, watching Harlan close. "I figure a man staring at the rope might be interested in other ways to spend his morning."

Harlan didn't speak right away.

Didn't rush.

He just studied McKinnrick, the way a man might study a snake sunning itself on a rock, trying to figure whether it'd strike if he got too close. The offer was easy enough to understand—ride with him, work for him, live. Simple on the surface. But Harlan knew better than to take things at face value. Nothing in this world came free. He shifted his weight, lifting his head slightly, his lip still split from the deputy's fist, his jaw sore. He could feel the weight of the night pressing down on him, feel the gallows standing somewhere beyond the stone walls, the rope waiting to bite the skin of his throat.

Harlan exhaled slow. "That a job offer?"

McKinnrick smirked. A slight thing, like a gambler who already knew he was holding the winning hand. "More of an invitation." He sat back again, his body relaxed, his voice steady. "You ride with me, earn your keep, you live." He tilted his head just slightly. "You say no... well, the sheriff's got his rope oiled and ready."

His meaning sat between them, heavy as the iron bars of the cell. McKinnrick wasn't begging him. He wasn't trying to convince him. He was laying out the facts, same as a dealer laying down a final card. And Harlan knew what that meant. The kind of man who gave ultimatums like this didn't lose sleep over whether a man lived or died. If Harlan took the offer, he was expected to pull his weight. If he refused, McKinnrick would watch him swing and move on without a second thought. That meant one thing for sure—McKinnrick was a man who could afford to lose him. Which meant he already had men. Which meant whatever Harlan was being offered, it wasn't just an act of kindness.

Harlan let out another slow breath, his fingers pressing lightly against the worn fabric of his pants. The cot creaked beneath him as he shifted slightly, the damp air of the jailhouse thick and unmoving. He didn't trust McKinnrick. But trust didn't have a damn thing to do with survival. He didn't answer right away. Just sat there, feeling the moment stretch. McKinnrick didn't rush him. Didn't push. He just waited, patient as a man who already knew which way the scales would tip.

McKinnrick stretched slow, rolling his shoulders like a man who had all the time in the world. The wooden chair creaked as he pushed himself up, his hands resting easy on his belt, just above the iron on his hip. "Well, I'd say you got a decision to make," he said, voice smooth, casual—like they were just passing time, not cutting a deal over a jail cell. He glanced toward the bars, then reached into his coat and pulled out a few silver coins, letting them clink against the rough wood of the sheriff's desk.

Sheriff Grady moved into view, he barely looked at them before scooping them up, making them disappear like they'd never been there at all.

So that's how it was.

Harlan had figured as much. A man like McKinnrick didn't bust down doors when he could buy his way through 'em.

Grady stood up, scratching at his thick, greying beard, then walked over and pulled the ring of keys from his belt.

"Looks like you're a free man," he muttered as he jammed a key into the lock.

The iron door groaned as it swung open.

McKinnrick smiled, just a little. "Congratulations, son. You're riding with the Rangers now."

Harlan felt his jaw go tight. "That so?"

McKinnrick gave a slow nod. "That's so."

But Harlan wasn't sure he believed that. Didn't much like the way Grady had taken the money and gone back to his desk without a single glance in his direction. He didn't trust either of these bastards. But he also wasn't about to stay in this cell.

Harlan stepped past Grady, grabbing his hat from where it hung on a nail by the door, brushing the dust from the brim before setting it back on his head.

McKinnrick watched him like a man who'd just won a hand he never had to bluff. "Come on, Ranger," he said with a smirk, turning for the door. "Got a ride ahead of us."

Harlan followed him out into the cool night. He could see the gallows waiting outside, could feel the noose that had been meant for him. And just like that, he left it behind. McKinnrick turned, leading the way. Harlan followed, his boots steady against the wood. Harlan kept close behind, his boots silent against the cold stone, his gun belt now slung low back on his hips, where it belonged. He didn't look back. Didn't see a reason to.

The night was bitter cold, the kind that sank into a man's bones and stayed there. Harlan pulled in a slow breath, letting it clear the stale air of the cell from his lungs. The town lay still, quiet as a graveyard. A few lamps burned dim behind shuttered windows, but no one dared look outside. Men who lived in places like this knew when to keep their heads down. The saloon was dark. The streets were empty.

And waiting just beyond the jailhouse, half-hidden in the shadows, were the horses. There were five of them, stamping restless against the dirt, their breath rising in thin plumes of mist. Their tack was good leather, bits polished, saddles well-worn but sturdy. These weren't stolen ponies. These were the kind of horses men rode when they expected to use them.

McKinnrick strode toward the biggest of the lot—a black stallion with a deep chest and sharp eyes. He grabbed the saddle horn, swung up in one smooth motion, and settled in like he belonged there. "Mount up."

That was it. No instructions, no questions. Just a command. Harlan didn't ask where they were going. Didn't need to. He grabbed the reins of a waiting buckskin, its ears flicking back at his touch. The horse was strong, well-muscled, its coat slick in the moonlight. Harlan ran a hand along its neck, feeling the tense power beneath the skin, then hauled himself up, his boots hitting the stirrups in one practiced motion. The leather creaked beneath him. The horse shifted slightly, testing his weight, but settled quick. He sat there for a moment, gripping the reins, feeling the chill sink through his coat. Then he turned his head—one last glance toward the town. Toward the jailhouse. Toward the gallows, standing quiet in the moonlight. It was still there. Still waiting. But it wasn't waiting for him. Not anymore. McKinnrick nudged his stallion forward, and Harlan didn't hesitate. He gave the buckskin a slight squeeze of the heels, and the horse moved beneath him, the hooves kicking up dust as they rode out—away from the gallows, away from whatever life had been waiting for him there.

The town faded behind them, shrinking into the distance, the lantern lights dimming as the streets fell away into desert scrub and hard-packed dirt. Above them, the first hints of dawn broke against the horizon, turning the sky the color of bruised iron. Harlan didn't know exactly what he was riding into. But he knew one thing. It sure as hell beat hanging.

CHAPTER 3: BLOOD ON THE BADGE

The desert stretched wide and empty, nothing but scrub and dry, cracked earth in every direction. The horizon lay distant, broken only by the jagged spines of mountains, their peaks still kissed with the dying chill of the night. The air was cool, but that wouldn't last. The sun was coming. Harlan could feel it rising behind him, slow but steady, its heat creeping across the land like a thing alive, burning away the last of the night's cold. Soon enough, the world would be sweltering, the dust rising thick beneath their horses, baking in the dry air.

For now, they rode in the quiet of the morning, the world hushed beneath the weight of dawn. Harlan rode a little behind McKinnrick, his buckskin moving smooth beneath him, hooves barely stirring the ground as they cut westward across the open land.

He didn't ask where they were going. Didn't need to. He was still feeling them out—the men, the pace, the way this outfit moved. And they moved like men with purpose. They weren't your usual gang of saddle bums and whiskey-bitten outlaws. These men carried themselves like soldiers.

They moved with discipline, not the reckless, greedy urgency of men chasing a score. They rode with the ease of those who had done it a hundred times before, men who knew their horses, knew their weapons, and knew how to use both.

They rode hard for the better part of the morning, stopping only when the sun had climbed high enough to turn the dust thick in their throats. McKinnrick finally raised a hand, signaling a halt near a shallow creek shaded by a thin cluster of mesquites. The water was low, the banks cracked and dry, but it was enough to let the horses drink and enough time for a quick pot of coffee. The men swung down from their saddles, stretching stiff limbs, some heading toward the fire one of McKinnrick's men had already built.

McKinnrick motioned for Harlan to follow. He walked toward the fire where the smell of strong coffee cut through the dust and sweat.

"Figured it's time you meet some of the boys proper," McKinnrick said. He gestured around the small clearing, where the riders were settling in, stretching sore limbs, rolling cigarettes. "Jonas Cutter," he said first, nodding to a man who sat apart from the others. Cutter was older than most, grizzled and sharp-eyed, with deep lines carved into his face from too much sun and too many long years on the trail. Harlan a single nod, nothing more.

"Dixon and Poe." McKinnrick turned toward two men crouched by the fire, passing a tin of tobacco between them. Dixon was broad-shouldered, thick through the arms, a man who looked like he'd rather use his fists than his gun. Poe, lean and sharp-featured, had the kind of smile that never quite reached his eyes.

"Dixon breaks bones, Poe just enjoys the work," McKinnrick said with a smirk.

Dixon grunted, stuffing a wad of tobacco into his cheek. "Long as it pays, don't matter much."

"And that sorry bastard over there is Kearney," McKinnrick continued, nodding toward a wiry young man who sat on his haunches, chewing on a strip of dried beef. "He talks too much, but he's quick with a knife."

Kearney grinned, flashing teeth, then tipped his hat. "Hope you're quicker with a gun, new blood."

Harlan only gave him a look, then took the tin cup of coffee Cutter handed him. The brew was thick, black as ink, and good. He drank it down slowly while McKinnrick introduced the rest of the men, letting the names settle in his mind, getting a feel for the men. They weren't ranch hands, they weren't ordinary gunmen. These men had the look of professionals—men who'd killed, men who'd survived. And now, he was one of them. Harlan took in the rest of the crew—men he hadn't been introduced to yet. There was a lean Mexican with sharp eyes and a silver-handled knife tucked at his hip, quiet as a ghost but always watching. A half-Indian with long black hair tied back, moving with the easy grace of a man used to slipping through the wild unnoticed. Half a dozen other riders, all of them capable-looking, the kind of men who didn't talk much and kept their business to themselves.

They weren't just hired guns. They were professionals. And that, more than anything, told Harlan that McKinnrick's outfit wasn't just some backwater gang.

The set out again shortly afterwards, to Harlan's left, Jonas Cutter rode with his hat low, chewing lazily on tobacco, the spent juice hitting the dirt every few minutes. His face was lined, his skin leathered by time and war, the grizzled stubble on his jaw blending into an old scar that ran from ear to chin. His six-shooter was strapped crosswise across his chest, not at his hip—a soldier's way of carrying a gun, fast to pull, easy to aim. He wasn't watching the land. He was watching Harlan.

Behind him, Vic Kearney, barely more than a kid, sat easy in the saddle, one leg hooked over the horn like he had nowhere in particular to be. But Harlan had seen the knife at his hip, the way his fingers drummed absently against the handle. Quick hands. Restless. The kind of boy who had too much blood in him, always looking for a way to spill it.

Hale Dixon rode just ahead, his broad frame hunched slightly forward in the saddle, thick arms gripping the reins. He was built like a bear, heavy in the gut, but not slow—not by the way his rifle was always within reach. His knuckles were thick with scars, healed over from too many beatings delivered, not taken.

And then there was Cyrus Poe.

Mean-eyed, sharp-featured, a smile that stretched a little too long and a little too easy. His rifle was cradled across his lap, but his hand never drifted far from the trigger. Harlan had met his kind before—men who didn't just kill when they had to, but because they wanted to. A cold thing settled in Harlan's gut. He'd killed men, but he never took joy in it. Cyrus Poe? He looked like he could laugh while pulling the trigger.

They rode hard, pushing across miles of open land, following no real trail. Just cutting westward, weaving between cacti and boulders, their hooves kicking up plumes of dust that stretched long behind them. The desert was waking. A hawk drifted overhead, silent, waiting. Lizards darted over sun-baked rock. Somewhere behind them, a coyote yipped a last call before slinking into its den.

Harlan kept quiet, but he listened. He watched. The way they spoke, the way they moved. They were comfortable with each other. This was a tight outfit, men who had been riding together for a while, who knew their place. And Harlan was the outsider. They didn't say it. Didn't have to. It was in the way Jonas Cutter's eyes lingered on him a second too long. The way Vic Kearney smirked whenever he glanced back at Harlan, like he was waiting for something to happen. The way Cyrus Poe occasionally turned his head, watching, like he was measuring something.

McKinnrick led without question. He sat tall in the saddle, his coat flaring slightly in the wind, his hat low over his eyes. The dust collected on his boots, on his shoulders, but he didn't seem to notice. Or maybe he just didn't care. The man rode like he owned the ground beneath him. And the others followed him without hesitation.

Harlan started picking up small details. The way Hale Dixon scanned the horizon without being told. The way Jonas Cutter's hand always rested near his gun, even when they were just riding. The way Cyrus Poe seemed to keep count of the miles, marking waypoints and pointing them out. This wasn't just a gang. This was a unit. Disciplined. Professional. McKinnrick had said they were rangers, but Harlan wasn't sure about that.

The sun rose higher, the heat building with every step, the air growing dry, dust caking in Harlan's throat. He rolled a cigarette, struck a match against his boot, and let the smoke curl between his lips. He wasn't sure where they were going. Didn't much matter. What mattered was figuring out just how deep in the dirt McKinnrick's boots were planted. And whether Harlan was willing to sink his own boots alongside them.

The wind whispered low through the sage and dry grass, carrying the faint scent of dust and desert bloom. The sky had bled out into deep indigo, the stars creeping in one by one, sharp and endless. They had made camp in a dry wash beneath a rocky ridge, the land cupped around them like a protective hand, shielding them from the worst of the wind. The fire flickered low, casting long, shifting shadows across the ground.

The men moved about in that slow, easy way of those who had done this a hundred times before—removing saddles, unslinging rifles, unbuckling belts heavy with iron. Boots off, backs against saddles, the scrape of flint on steel as Cutter struck a fire, the glow catching in the hollows of their faces. A whiskey bottle was making the rounds. Harlan kept to himself, rolling a smoke, letting the conversation drift around him like campfire smoke. He had learned a long time ago that in a group like this, a man was better off listening first, talking second.

The bottle landed in Cutter's hands, and the old soldier took a long pull, wiped his mouth on the back of his sleeve, then leaned forward, the fire catching the deep creases in his face. "You boys ever hear about the raid on Baxter's Crossing?" Cutter asked, his voice low and rough, thick with the kind of satisfaction that came from knowing he had a good story to tell.

Vic Kearney grinned, his eyes glinting in the firelight. "That the one where you ran with Quantrill's Raiders?"

Cutter chuckled, chewing his tobacco slow. He leaned back against his saddle, his body loose, relaxed, but his hand still resting near the revolver strapped crosswise across his chest. "Maybe," he said. "Maybe not."

Vic let out a laugh, shaking his head. "Damn, Cutter. Either you was there or you wasn't."

Cutter spat into the dirt, his grin showing yellowed teeth. "Ain't the point, kid. Ain't about what's true. It's about what folks believe."

That got a low murmur of agreement from Dixon, who sat with his legs stretched out, his boots near the fire, his fingers absently running over the stock of his rifle. Across the fire, Cyrus Poe had his knife out, the steel catching the light as he slowly worked the blade over a whetstone, the rhythm steady, almost hypnotic. The sound of it scraped through the night.

"You boys waste too much time with stories," Poe muttered. "Only thing that matters is how fast you pull iron when it counts."

Vic smirked. "That so? You ever have to test that theory?"

Poe's eyes didn't lift from his knife. "Three men outside Santa Fe. They thought they had the drop on me."

He let the words sit there, hanging between them like the smoke curling from Harlan's cigarette. The others didn't react much. No shock. No real interest. Just the same easy, comfortable nods a man gives when hearing about a trip to the general store. That was what sat wrong with Harlan. The fact that these men laughed like it was a campfire tale and not a confession.

McKinnrick hadn't said much all night, just leaned back against a boulder, legs stretched out, his eyes half-lidded like he was resting but still listening. The firelight flickered against the hard planes of his face, carving deep shadows beneath his brow, catching the silver strands in his hair.

Harlan could feel his eyes on him before the man even spoke. "You ever wear a badge?" McKinnrick asked.

The conversation stilled, just for a beat. Not a silence. But a shift. Even Cutter stopped chewing for a second, his jaw tightening just a little before he took another sip from the whiskey bottle.

Harlan took his time, exhaling smoke, tapping the ash loose from the end of his cigarette. "Not the type they pin on."

McKinnrick studied him, his expression unreadable. Then, slow, he nodded. "Most badges don't mean much anyway."

That was the end of it. The bottle kept moving. The conversation picked up again. Vic cracked a joke. Cutter laughed. Poe kept sharpening his blade. But Harlan wasn't paying attention to them anymore. He was watching McKinnrick. The fire crackled low, sending embers curling into the night air. Shadows stretched long over the hard-packed earth, the heat barely holding back the chill settling in from the desert beyond the ridge. The smell of burnt coffee, horse sweat, and damp leather hung in the air, the usual stench of men who'd spent too many miles in the saddle.

Harlan sat across from McKinnrick, rolling a cigarette slow between his fingers, thinking. He'd been running with these men long enough now to get a feel for them, but there was something about McKinnrick that he couldn't quite pin down.

The man was careful. Too careful.

Didn't talk much unless it was worth talking about.

So that made this question worth asking.

Harlan struck a match, let the flame catch on the end of the cigarette, then exhaled slow.

"Why me?"

McKinnrick glanced up from where he was cleaning his revolver, rubbing a rag along the cylinder, slow and methodical. His expression didn't shift, but Harlan saw it—the small flicker of amusement in his eyes, like he'd been waiting for the question.

"Two men down," McKinnrick said, voice low and even.

Harlan said nothing, just let the words settle, waiting for the rest.

McKinnrick flipped the revolver shut with a soft click, resting it on his knee.

"Jess Holden and Budge caught the wrong end of a bullet in a damn fool bar fight," he went on. "Whiskey got in 'em too deep, and next thing you know, some ranch hand puts a slug in Holden's belly. Budge goes to help, gets himself shot clean through the skull. Just like that, I'm two men short."

Harlan took another slow drag, watching the firelight shift in McKinnrick's eyes. "So you decided to bust me outta jail?"

McKinnrick smirked. He leaned back against his saddle, crossing one boot over the other. "I'd heard about you. Heard about that shootout."

Harlan stiffened just a little, but kept his face still.

"Asked a few questions," McKinnrick continued. "It was West Gage, the rancher, said it was a fair fight. Said you outdrew the drifter. Clean. Fast."

Harlan let that sit.

West Gage. He hadn't expected to hear that name again. Gage had been the only one that night who hadn't looked at him like he was another low-down killer.

McKinnrick reached for his flask, twisted off the top, and took a slow sip.

"Said he knew you worked the drives. That you were handy with an iron." He shrugged. "I could use a man like that."

He passed the flask to Harlan. Harlan took it, but didn't drink right away. He just sat there, letting the words turn over in his head.

The rancher had called it a fair fight.

The law sure as hell hadn't.

The law had left him to hang for it.

Harlan took a long swallow from the flask, letting the burn work its way down. Maybe McKinnrick had done him a favor. Or maybe he'd just traded one kind of trouble for another.

The fire had burned low, red embers pulsing in the pit, sending up the occasional spark into the night air. The others had started turning in—Poe snoring against his saddle, Dixon half-drunk but still upright, muttering to himself as he nursed a bottle.

McKinnrick had wandered off to check the horses, leaving the camp in a hush, the kind that settled after a long day of hard riding.

Harlan sat a little apart from the rest, boots stretched toward the dying fire, rolling a smoke between his fingers. The paper crinkled as he worked, slow and deliberate, letting the quiet soak into his bones. He was still getting used to these men, still figuring out where he fit in among them, if he even did.

A shadow moved in the firelight, then Cutter lowered himself onto a nearby log. He pulled a tobacco pouch from his pocket, shook out a pinch, and offered it over with a flick of his wrist. A small gesture, but one that said more than words.

Harlan nodded, and the offering. "Appreciate it."

Cutter struck a match and lit his own smoke, taking a slow drag, eyes half-lidded as he exhaled. "Long day," he said after a moment, his voice rough from years of dust and cigarettes.

Harlan nodded. "Been worse."

Cutter gave a dry chuckle. "Yeah. Been worse."

For a while, they just sat there, the only sound the low pop of the fire and the faint wind whispering through the sage. Then Cutter spoke again, his voice quieter this time.

"Rode with the cavalry for a spell," he said, tapping ash into the dirt. "Before the war ended. Thought I was doin' something important. Thought I was part of something bigger than myself."

Harlan glanced at him but said nothing, letting him talk.

"Turns out, we were just bodies on horses, throwin' ourselves at bullets for men who didn't give a damn about us." Cutter took another pull from his cigarette. "Saw good men get cut down in the mud, and for what? A piece of land they'd never see again? A name in some officer's book?" He shook his head. "Ain't much honor in dyin' for a cause that don't care if you're dead or not."

Harlan let that settle before he spoke. "I didn't fight in the war. Too young when it started, I guess. Spent most of my time pushing cattle, working drives. Just another saddle tramp looking for pay."

Cutter studied him through the haze of smoke, his eyes sharp but not unkind. "Ain't many honest livin's left these days," he said. "You either swing a shovel or a gun."

Harlan thought on that, rolling his cigarette between his fingers before taking a slow drag. The words stuck with him, sinking deep. "Guess I ain't much for shovels," he said.

Cutter smirked, exhaling smoke. "Then you're in the right place."

The fire crackled, the moment stretching between them, quiet but understood. For the first time, Harlan felt something close to belonging.

It wasn't much. But it was something.

CHAPTER 4: RIDING FOR THE LAW

The town was just another speck in the dust, barely holding itself together—a cluster of buildings warped by sun and wind, the streets rutted with wagon tracks, the air thick with the scent of horses and dry earth. Harlan rode in beside McKinnrick, watching as the townsfolk took notice. Eyes flicked their way—some curious, some wary, a few relieved.

McKinnrick rode like a man with a claim on the land beneath him. Loose in the saddle, his coat hanging open just enough to show the shine of a six-pointed badge, but not enough to make it clear which side of the law it belonged to, he just flashed it when the moment called for it, and men believed what they wanted to.

A heavyset man stepped forward as they reined in, his coat stretched tight across his broad frame, the gold chain of a pocket watch glinting in the evening sun. His collar was stiff, his boots polished, but there was sweat beading at his temples, darkening the fabric beneath his arms. A judge, maybe a mayor. The kind of man who was used to holding authority in a place that barely had any—but right now, standing in front of McKinnrick and his men, he didn't look so sure of it.

McKinnrick swung down from his horse, boots kicking up dust as he stepped forward. He pulled off his gloves slow, shaking out the heat from the ride, looking like a man without a single concern.

"You McKinnrick?" the official asked, voice tight.

McKinnrick gave a small nod, like his name didn't need saying twice. "You must be Mayor Goode?"

Goode nodded exhaled hard, relief warring with unease on his face. "Glad you made it."

McKinnrick took his time dusting off his hat. "You got a problem," he said, like he was discussing the weather.

The mayor nodded. "Yeah I do. His name's Jonah Phelps. Been robbing stagecoaches, killed a lawman in the next town over. Bastard's got himself holed up in the hills. Sherrif Howdon took a hit to his gut and his deputy, Sam Sinton, got a shattered knee from one of Phelp's bullets "

McKinnrick smiled—just a flicker of teeth, quick and easy. "That's why we're here."

Harlan didn't move right away. Didn't dismount. Didn't speak. Just sat in the saddle and watched.

There was something about the way McKinnrick handled the exchange. How the mayor didn't question him. Didn't ask for paperwork or proof. How the men in their group carried themselves—not like deputies, not like a posse. They were too loose, too at ease, not men bound by rules, but by something else entirely. A real lawman would've been clear about his authority. McKinnrick didn't have to be. He let the badge do the talking.

The sun was high and merciless by the time they left town, following an old mining road winding into the hills. Dust kicked up from their horses' hooves, clinging to sweat-damp shirts, mixing with the dry tang of sage and rock.

McKinnrick led them like he already knew the way. Poe and Dixon rode close behind, their eyes scanning the ridges. Harlan kept back, watching more than listening.

They found the shack just before sundown. A sagging wooden structure, leaning against the rocks like it was just waiting for the wind to take it down. McKinnrick signaled them to stop, holding up his hand. They split off—Dixon and Cutter flanking left, Poe circling wide. Harlan eased his revolver from its holster, the weight familiar in his grip.

Inside the shack, a single lantern flickered. A shadow passed behind the warped slats of wood.

McKinnrick gave the kind of smile that didn't reach his eyes. "Show's over, Phelps."

The gunfire came fast and desperate. The first shot ripped through the stillness, shattering the quiet. Then all hell broke loose. Phelps fired from inside, bullets chewing up the wooden walls, kicking up splinters. Dixon returned fire, sending rounds snapping through the doorway.

Poe let out a sharp laugh as he dropped low, firing through a gap in the planks. "Ain't nowhere to run, Phelps!"

Inside, footsteps pounded—fast, uneven. Harlan saw the back door slam open, saw Phelps bolt into the brush. McKinnrick barely hesitated. Didn't call for surrender. Didn't tell him to stop.

Dixon raised his rifle. One shot.

Phelps grunted, stumbled—clutching his gut as his knees hit the dirt. The fight was over. Phelps twitched once, blood pooling beneath him. He lifted his head just enough to see McKinnrick standing over him, silhouetted against the dying sun. McKinnrick squatted, tilting his head. "Told you, Jonah. Show's over."

Phelps tried to say something, but it came out wet. Didn't matter.

McKinnrick straightened. "Bag him up."

Dixon wiped his mouth with the back of his hand, then spit into the dirt.

"Easy money."

Harlan exhaled slow.

Easy money.

The sun hung low when they rode back into town, Jonah Phelps' lifeless body slung over the back of Dixon's horse, dust rising from the dry road as the bloodied corpse swayed with the motion of the horse.

By the time they hit the main street, people had already gathered. News traveled fast out here— faster than a bullet, sometimes. Men and women spilled out of buildings, stepping off boardwalks, watching with wide, eager eyes.

They'd been waiting for this.

Mayor Goode stood in the middle of the street, hands on his hips, eyes locked on Phelps' corpse. McKinnrick swung down from his saddle slow, stretching like a man who had all the time in the world. He reached for his flask, took a pull, and passed it to Dixon, who wiped the back of his hand across his mouth before taking a drink himself.

Harlan didn't move right away.

He stayed in the saddle, his grip on the reins loose, his eyes on the scene playing out before him.

McKinnrick strolled up to the mayor like they were old friends, extending his hand, clasping the man's wrist. "There's your problem solved, Goode."

Goode looked at Phelps' limp, dust-covered body, his face obscured with blood and grunted. "That him?"

McKinnrick smirked. "Unless you got another Jonah Phelps that needed killin'."

A ripple of chuckles passed through the gathered crowd, a few men clapping their hats against their thighs.

"You and your men did good, McKinnrick," the mayor said, nodding. "Mighty good."

McKinnrick's smile never faded. "Ain't that what we do?"

He clapped Goode on the shoulder, shook the mayor's hand, smiled easy, talking in that slow, sure voice of his. He played it well, Harlan had to admit. Like a real lawman. Harlan wondered if maybe he'd been wrong about all of it. Maybe this was the right side of things. Maybe this wasn't as bad as he'd thought it might be.

The saloon was alive with noise, laughter, the clink of glasses and the shuffle of boots on the floorboards. McKinnrick's boys held court at the biggest table in the room. Dixon had a woman in his lap, grinning through whiskey-stained teeth as he slapped coins down onto the poker table. Poe leaned back in his chair, flipping his knife between his fingers. Cutter was already half-drunk, recounting the moment Phelps caught the bullet, shaking his head like it was the best damn thing he'd seen all week. The drinks were free tonight, the mayor made sure of that. They'd done their job. They'd been paid. They were heroes. Harlan sat a little further back, his glass half-full, watching. McKinnrick had talked about riding with the Rangers. And maybe—just maybe—he really was.

Maybe this was what the law looked like out here. Rough, bloody, but necessary. Harlan turned his glass slow in his hand, watching the way the lamplight caught the amber whiskey inside.

The saloon doors swung open with a slow, deliberate creak, cutting through the smoke-thick air like a blade. The easy murmur of conversation hitched for half a second, then picked up again as men glanced toward the entrance and recognized the figure stepping inside.

McKinnrick, shoulders squared, his coat swinging open just enough to show the holstered iron on his hip. He took his time crossing the floor, boots knocking steady against the warped planks, eyes sweeping the room like he was taking inventory of what belonged to him.

Harlan watched him approach, halfway through a hand of cards, whiskey burning slow in his gut. McKinnrick didn't look at him right away. Instead, he stopped at the bar, tossing down a few heavy coins that clinked against the worn wood. "Bottle," he said, voice even, like he wasn't making a request.

The barkeep moved fast, setting down a fresh bottle and a handful of shot glasses. McKinnrick turned to face the room, his mouth curving into something like a smile. "Figure it's about time you boys got paid."

That got their attention.

Dixon and Poe stopped mid-conversation, grinning like they'd been waiting for it all night. Cutter leaned forward, eyes sharp with interest.

McKinnrick started passing out coins like a man distributing favors.

"Dixon." He tossed coins his way. "For the shot that put Phelps in the dirt."

Dixon caught the money one-handed, grinning as it disappeared into his vest pocket.

"Poe." Another few coins. "For making sure that bastard stayed down."

Poe chuckled, raising his whiskey glass in silent appreciation before tucking the money into his coat.

McKinnrick turned to Harlan last. "And you, Harlan," he said, his voice steady, unreadable.

Harlan blinked, caught off guard. He hadn't expected payment. Hell, he hadn't even thought about it.

McKinnrick smirked at the look on his face, tilting his head slightly. "You rode with me, didn't you? You helped put a wanted man in the ground." He tossed the coins onto the table. "You earned it."

Harlan let the moment stretch, the weight of McKinnrick's words settling over him.

Then, slowly, he reached out, picked up the money. Now he was sitting at a table with a full whiskey glass, fresh money in his pocket, and the kind of easy satisfaction that came from knowing he'd live to see another night.

Maybe, for now, that was enough.

McKinnrick tipped his hat slightly, then turned back toward the bar. "Now drink up, boys. It's been a good day."

And just like that, the saloon roared back to life. The saloon was thick with cigar smoke, the air warm with sweat, whiskey, and the low murmur of voices. Lamps flickered against the polished wood of the bar, casting long shadows across the floorboards. The place wasn't fancy, but it had enough whiskey and enough cards to make a man forget his troubles for a night.

Harlan sat at a round table near the back, leaning easy in his chair, one boot hooked over the rung as he studied his hand. Five-card draw. A few coins already sat in the middle of the pot, gleaming dull under the yellow light.

Across from him, Dixon chewed on an unlit cigar, tapping his cards against the table like he was waiting for 'em to change. Cutter sat next to him, his face unreadable as he scanned the table.

Poe, the mean-eyed bastard, grinned wide as he shuffled his coins, watching Harlan like a snake waiting to strike. "Reckon you got somethin', Harlan?" he asked, voice lazy but sharp.

Harlan smirked, took a slow sip of whiskey. "Reckon we'll see, won't we?"

The whiskey was better than he expected—not great, but warm enough in the gut. And after the long ride, after the shootout, after dragging Phelps into town, it tasted damn near perfect.

Dixon let out a grunt, tossing a few coins into the pot. "Too rich for me," he muttered, folding.

Cutter tossed in a few more coins. "Call."

Poe studied Harlan a second longer, then matched the bet.

All eyes landed on him.

Harlan flicked his gaze to the pot, then to Poe, then back down to his hand. A queen, a jack, and a pair of eights. Not a great hand, but enough.

He threw in a few more coins, just enough to keep 'em guessing.

Poe's grin widened. "Hell, son. You must be feelin' lucky."

Cutter dealt the last round of cards.

Harlan lifted the corner of his new card, slow, deliberate. An ace.

Poe exhaled through his nose, cracked his knuckles, then pushed the rest of his coins into the pot. "All in."

Dixon chuckled low, watching the play unfold. Cutter didn't so much as blink. Harlan turned his glass between his fingers, thinking. He'd played enough hands in enough rough saloons to know when a man was bluffing. And Poe? He liked to grin too much when he had nothin'. Harlan smirked and matched the bet.

Cutter sighed, shook his head. "Damn fools, both of you." He tossed his cards in.

Poe laid his hand down with a flourish. A pair of tens. He leaned back, spreading his arms like he was already spending his winnings. "Ain't much, but it's enough."

Harlan placed his hand down slow, tapping the ace with two fingers. "Not quite."

For a moment, the table went quiet.

Then Dixon let out a bark of laughter. "Ain't that a damn thing."

Poe's grin faded. His lip curled, and for a second, Harlan thought he might reach for his knife. But then he exhaled, grumbling as he tossed his cigar stub onto the table. "Lucky son of a bitch."

Harlan smirked, scooped the pot toward him, stacking the coins in neat little piles.

Cutter chuckled. "Don't let him win too much, Poe, or you'll be drinkin' well water the rest of the night."

Poe shook his head but didn't press it further. The man didn't like losing, but he knew better than to stir up a fight over a card game. Harlan leaned back in his chair, whiskey warming his chest, the weight of a few extra dollars in his pocket.

The company was rough, sure—but hell, he was used to that. From the trail, from the drives, from the men who spent their lives between the dust and the saloons, chasing paydays and bad decisions. And for the first time he didn't feel like a man on the run. He was just a man with a good hand, a full glass, and a long night ahead of him.

The game stretched long into the night, the whiskey burning smoother with each pour, the laughter at the table growing easier. Harlan had played enough hands in enough saloons to know when to call it quits, and tonight, he was leaving the table on the right side of luck.

The pile of coins in front of him felt damn good. Enough for a room. Enough for a woman. Enough to let him forget, just for one night, the miles he'd put behind him.

Poe was licking his wounds after losing too many hands, throwing back whiskey like it might dull the sting of it. Cutter had left the table already, wandering toward the bar. Dixon had started a fresh cigar, the tip glowing in the low lamplight, watching the next round of players settle in.

Harlan gave the pile of coins in front of him a slow, measured glance, then tapped his knuckles on the wood. "That's me done."

Poe grunted, rolling his shoulders. "You got any damn sense, you'd stay. Bet them winnings proper."

Harlan smirked, scooping up the money and pocketing it. "Reckon I'll spend it proper instead."

That got a chuckle from Dixon, who knocked back another mouthful of whiskey before shaking his head. "Ain't no such thing as proper in a place like this."

Harlan just smiled, stood from the table, and stretched. The saloon was warm, thick with the scent of stale liquor and too many bodies crammed into one place. The floor creaked beneath his boots, the air humming with voices and the occasional burst of laughter from a far-off corner.

He took a glance around. Most of McKinnrick's men were still drinking, still playing, still holding court at the center of the room.

He didn't have to watch his back here.

Not tonight.

He felt safe.

Upstairs, the hallway smelled of perfume and candle wax, the flickering lamplight casting long shadows against the faded wallpaper. The floor creaked beneath his boots as he walked, passing closed doors, muffled laughter, the soft murmur of conversation behind them.

A woman leaned against the doorway of one of the rooms, her dress loose at the shoulders, dark curls framing a face that had seen plenty but still carried a kind of easy charm. She looked him over as he stopped, her gaze sharp but playful. "You looking for a bed, cowboy?"

Harlan let the weight of the coins in his pocket settle against his palm before he smirked. "Looking for a warm one."

She grinned, pushing the door open a little wider, stepping back just enough to invite him in. The room was small but comfortable, the bed made up with sheets that had seen better days, but they were clean, and right now, that was enough. The woman moved easy, stepping closer with the kind of confidence that came from knowing exactly what a man needed when he walked into a place like this. She reached for his hat first, sliding it off slow, brushing her fingers through his hair. Then his coat, easing it from his shoulders.

She stood close enough for him to catch the faint scent of rosewater and something sweeter underneath, something warm and womanly, something that wrapped around him like a second skin.

Her fingers went to the buttons of his shirt, undoing them slow, deliberate. She didn't rush, and he didn't stop her. Didn't want to.

He was just a man in a quiet room, with soft hands tracing old scars, a warm mouth pressing against his throat, and the simple need to forget. He let her push the shirt from his shoulders, let her lips find his, let the heat between them pull him under, wipe out the last few days like they never happened.

Because right now, this was the only thing that felt real.

And he needed real more than he'd ever needed anything.

Not the trail.

Not the fights.

Not McKinnrick.

Just this.

Much later, when the lamplight burned low and the saloon noise faded beneath them, Harlan lay back against the mattress, his arms folded behind his head. The woman was curled against his side, fingers idly tracing the ridges of an old scar along his ribs.

"You stayin' long?" she asked, voice thick with sleep.

He stared up at the ceiling, exhaled slow. "Don't reckon so."

She made a small sound, something between a sigh and disappointment. She'd heard that before. Probably too many times.

He turned his head slightly, watching the way her lashes flickered against her cheek, the way her breathing slowed, easy, like she wasn't thinking too hard about what kind of man had come through her door tonight.

A safe bed. A warm body. A pocket full of coin. Harlan let himself close his eyes without worrying what waited on the other side of sleep.

CHAPTER 5: A JUST CAUSE

Perdition Wells was little more than a wide stretch of dirt road lined with wooden buildings, the kind of place that had grown out of necessity rather than ambition. A saloon with a faded sign leaned against its own support beams, a general store stood with its shutters half-open, and a squat sheriff's office sat beside a small corral. Further down, ranch houses and outbuildings sprawled into open cattle country, the land golden under the late afternoon sun.

The gang rode slow into town, the dust from their journey still clinging to their coats, their horses breathing heavy from the hard miles behind them. Harlan kept a steady grip on the reins, scanning the faces that peered from doorways and windows.

They were being watched, but not with suspicion.

With hope.

The town had been waiting for them.

At the center of the street, two men stood side by side, both looking like they hadn't slept in days.

The first was a thick-built man with a neatly trimmed beard, a waistcoat stretched tight across his frame—Mayor Jed Morrow. The second, leaner, with a tin star pinned to his chest and a rifle slung over his shoulder, was Sheriff Lane.

McKinnrick pulled his horse up in front of them and swung down in an easy motion, dusting off his coat as he stepped forward.

"You the men that sent word?" McKinnrick asked, his voice even, calm.

Mayor Morrow nodded quickly. "We are." He glanced past McKinnrick, taking in the rest of the riders with an anxious eye. "I hope you brought enough men."

McKinnrick smirked. "That depends. How many sons of bitches are we dealing with?"

The sheriff stepped forward, his face drawn tight. "Lyle Brothers. Seven or eight, maybe more. They move quick, strike at night, hit the ranches, run off cattle, leave the hands bleeding out in the dust."

Harlan felt the shift in the air.

He glanced at the others. Dixon rubbed a hand over his jaw, Poe cocked his head like he was already sizing up the job.

"They killed anyone?" McKinnrick asked.

The mayor swallowed. "Couple of ranchers. A boy too young to be caught up in this."

The words sat heavy in the space between them.

Harlan knew that was all McKinnrick needed to hear.

The old ranger straightened his coat, nodding slow, the weight of command settling into his stance.

"You hired the right men."

The mayor let out a breath like he'd been holding it too long.

"Thank God for that."

The trail led them out of Perdition Wells and into the hard country beyond, where the land was mean and dry, cut through with narrow canyons and jagged ridges, places a man could disappear if he knew how to use them.

They rode single file through the brush, the sun sitting low but still throwing heat off the rocks. The air smelled of dust and sage, the only sound the steady clop of hooves and the occasional creak of saddle leather.

Harlan rode a little off to the side, scanning the landscape as they followed the trail of trampled brush, cattle tracks, and boot prints heading into the hills. The Lyle Brothers weren't being careful—they weren't even trying to hide their path. Men like that thought they were untouchable.

That was about to change. This was the kind of work that made sense. Just men bringing killers to justice. Harlan exhaled slow, adjusting the brim of his hat against the sinking sun. Yeah, this felt right.

Up ahead, Dixon spit into the dust. "Reckon them bastards are in for a surprise."

Poe chuckled, rolling his shoulders. "I hope they run. Makes it more fun."

Cutter grinned. "Ain't no way this ends quiet. Lyles don't seem like the surrendering type."

Harlan didn't say much. He just kept his eyes on the trail, his hand resting easy on the grip of his revolver. They were hunting killers.

The sun hung low, its dying light stretching long shadows across the canyon floor. The rustlers had made camp in the narrow cut between the rocks, their fires burning low, pots bubbling with what passed for supper. Their stolen cattle were penned against a rock face, grazing lazily on what little grass there was. A few men sat near the flames, passing a bottle between them, their laughter echoing against the canyon walls.

They had no idea what was coming.

McKinnrick raised a fist, signaling for silence. The gang reined in their horses, their movements slow, controlled. Harlan slid from his saddle, boots hitting the dirt without a sound. He moved carefully, keeping to the shadows of the boulders, his revolver loose in its holster.

Dixon and Poe split off, taking higher ground along the ridge. Cutter flanked wide, eyes sharp beneath the brim of his hat.

The wind shifted, carrying the scent of burning wood and something greasy cooking in an iron pan. The rustlers were easy, comfortable. They thought they were safe.

They were wrong.

McKinnrick stepped forward, just enough to let his voice carry. "Clint Lyle!"

The laughter died.

The men at the fire snapped their heads up, hands pausing mid-motion, their bodies going tight. For a long moment, the only sound was the slow pop of the burning logs.

Then, movement.

Hands drifted toward their guns.

McKinnrick didn't move. Didn't even flinch.

"You boys are riding stolen cattle and running from a rope," he continued, his voice calm but edged with iron. "You put your hands up, and maybe you see a judge instead of a pine box."

One of the rustlers—a wiry man with a scar running from his ear to his jaw—swore under his breath. His fingers twitched toward the revolver on his hip.

McKinnrick's voice dropped lower. "I wouldn't."

Then Clint Lyle stepped out of the shadows. He was tall, broad across the shoulders, his dark hair hanging loose around a face that had been carved by too many hard years and bad choices. He had the look of a man who'd killed and never thought twice about it.

"This some kind of joke?" Lyle smirked, spreading his arms. "You boys think you're lawmen?"

McKinnrick didn't smile. Didn't move. "Ain't no joke."

The moment stretched too long, too tight. Then Lyle's hand shot toward his gun. Harlan didn't even think. His Colt was in his grip before he knew it, hammer cocked, ready—

The first shot cracked the silence, Harlan's bullet slamming into Lyle's shoulder sending him reeling backward.

Then all hell broke loose. Gunfire erupted. Two more rustlers pulled iron, but Dixon and Poe were faster. Their rifles cracked from the ridge, dropping one man before he could clear leather. The other stumbled back, blood spreading across his chest before he crumpled into the dirt. Another rustler tried to run—Cutter put a bullet in his leg, dropping him hard.

The rest? They threw up their hands.

Lyle coughed, groaning in the dirt, his gun lost somewhere in the dust, his hand to the hole in his shoulder. Before he could push himself up, McKinnrick was on him. He grabbed Lyle by the collar, hauled him up to his knees, their faces inches apart.

"You're done," McKinnrick said, his voice even, but there was no mistaking the finality in it.

Lyle spat blood into the dirt, his breath ragged. "Guess we'll see."

McKinnrick just smiled, but there wasn't a damn bit of warmth in it. "Yeah. I guess we will."

The saloon in Perdition Wells wasn't much— just a low-ceilinged, smoke-hazed room with rough-hewn tables and a long, scarred bar—but tonight, it felt like the grandest hall in the West. The bottles lining the shelves caught the flickering lamplight, and the air was thick with the scent of spilled whiskey, smoke, and sweat. The piano player hammered out a tune in the corner, more enthusiasm than skill, but no one seemed to mind.

McKinnrick's men had claimed a table near the center, their voices loud, their boots kicked up, their pockets heavier than they'd been in weeks. The job had paid well. And men who rode hard liked to spend hard.

Harlan leaned back in his chair, nursing a drink as the conversation rolled around him. His body ached from the long ride, from the tension of the fight, but it was a good ache. The kind that came from a job well done.

Across the table, Dixon let out a sharp laugh, slapping his hand against the wood. "Did you see that bastard's face when Harlan put a bullet in his shoulder? Damn near pissed himself."

Poe chuckled, rolling a cigarette between his fingers. "They always talk big right up until they're eating dirt." He struck a match, lighting the smoke with a slow drag before exhaling.

McKinnrick was standing at the bar, speaking low with the mayor. A small, leather-bound bag of coin sat between them. A payout for a service rendered. The mayor looked grateful, relieved even. Men like him—men who ran towns—couldn't afford to be picky about the hands that did their dirty work.

McKinnrick lifted the bag, weighing it in his palm before flicking it open and counting the coins inside. Then, satisfied, he nodded and turned back toward his men. McKiddrick walked through the haze of cigar smoke like he owned the place. There was an ease in his step, a quiet confidence in his expression. He looked like a man who'd never once doubted that today would end with him standing, with coin in his pocket and whiskey waiting.

"Hell of a job, boys," he said, setting the bag down on the table with a solid *thud*. He reached in, pulling out coins, tossing them toward each man.

Harlan caught his share, the silver cold in his palm. It wasn't much, but it was honest. At least, it felt that way.

"You earned it," McKinnrick said, meeting Harlan's gaze.

Harlan nodded, flipping one of the coins between his fingers. McKinnrick reached for the bottle of whiskey Cutter had claimed from the bar and poured heavy into each man's glass. When he was done, he raised his own. "To good work."

The men lifted their drinks, and the glasses clinked together in the dim light. Harlan took a slow sip, letting the burn settle in his gut.

The town had thanked them. The law had shaken their hands. They were getting paid and drinking like kings. The saloon was alive with heat and noise, whiskey sloshing in glasses, voices raised in half-drunken celebration. A job well done meant a night well spent, and the gang had taken their usual places—McKinnrick off in the corner talking business with some town official, while the rest of them settled in for a night of drinking, gambling, and whatever else their coin could buy.

Harlan sat at a round table near the back, watching as Cutter shuffled the deck with smooth, practiced hands. Dixon leaned back in his chair, a cigarette dangling from his lips, his eyes flicking between the cards and the bottle of whiskey on the table. Poe was already on his third drink, grinning like he had money to burn.

"Ante up, boys," Cutter said, voice easy as he slid the deck across the table.

Harlan tossed in a few coins, same as the others. The night was young, and he wasn't about to let himself get reckless.

Cutter dealt slow, his fingers steady, his expression unreadable. He wasn't the kind to play flashy, but Harlan could tell he'd been around a deck long enough to know the game better than most. Poe, on the other hand, played like he was trying to impress the damn cards, tossing his bets in too fast, too eager. Dixon played mean, staring down the others, waiting for them to flinch.

Harlan played careful. And Cutter? Cutter played like a man who'd learned the hard way that every dollar counted.

They went around the table, bets growing, whiskey flowing. Harlan kept his face steady, watching the men as much as the game. He saw the way Poe's confidence wavered when he raised too high. The way Dixon's fingers tapped against the table when he was bluffing. The way Cutter never once hesitated, keeping his movements deliberate, controlled.

The pot grew. Silver coins and folded bills piled in the center. The air tightened.

Dixon leaned forward, his grin sharp. "Reckon you got the cards for it, Cutter?"

Cutter just smirked, didn't answer right away. He flicked his eyes to Harlan instead. "What about you, kid? You feeling lucky?"

Harlan glanced at his cards—good, but not good enough. He exhaled slow, then laid them down. "Not tonight."

Cutter chuckled, nodding. "You got sense, kid. That'll keep you alive longer than your gun."

The round went on without him, Dixon and Poe pushing hard, but when the dust settled, Cutter raked in the pot, stacking his winnings neat, like he was in no rush to spend them.

Harlan reached for his whiskey, but before he could take a sip, a silver coin came sliding across the table, stopping near his hand.

He looked up. Cutter raised his glass. "Next drink's on me."

Harlan picked up the coin, rolling it between his fingers. He'd spent most of his life around men who were only looking out for themselves. But Cutter? Cutter wasn't trying to one-up him, wasn't looking to prove a damn thing.

It was just a small gesture.

But in this world, small gestures meant something.

Harlan tipped his hat, lifting his glass in return. "I'll drink to that."

The whiskey burned smooth down his throat, but for the first time in a while, it didn't taste like just another night in another saloon. It tasted like camaraderie.

CHAPTER 6: THE HUNT FOR JED ROYCE

The evening light stretched long across the land as McKinnrick sat astride his horse, one hand resting easy on the saddle horn, the other holding a folded scrap of paper. He'd been quiet since the rider had come through earlier, carrying news from a sheriff down in Silent Creek. Now, the fire flickered low, shadows dancing across the men as they waited.

McKinnrick finally spoke, his voice calm, steady. "Name's Jed Royce. Wanted in three counties. Murder, robbery. Been making a habit of taking what ain't his and leaving bodies in his wake."

He passed the paper to Poe, who smirked as he scanned the brief description. "Hell of a list," Poe muttered, flicking the paper over to Dixon.

McKinnrick didn't smile. "He's riding under an alias. We got a rough description—tall, wiry, dark hair. He's planning on take the stage at Sutterville heading for Red Bluff."

Harlan exhaled slow, nodding. This felt right. A man wanted for murder, a known outlaw. Another job that needed doing.

Cutter adjusted his hat, flipping open his pocket watch like always. "This straight from the law?"

McKinnrick gave a slow nod. "Sheriff wanted him brought back alive, but I figure dead'll do just as well." His eyes scanned the men around the fire. "We ride at first light."

The group exchanged glances, and Harlan caught a flicker of something in Cutter's expression—maybe doubt, maybe something else—but no one spoke against it.

McKinnrick stretched his back. "Dixon, Poe—you take the ridge overlooking the road. I want eyes on that coach before it even knows we're there." He turned to Cutter. "Cutter, you hang back, cover us with the other men," McKinnrick's eyes found his, steady, unreadable. "We pull him off the stage, make sure he's the right man, and bring him back." A pause, then he found Harlan's eyes. "Reckon you can ride with me," McKinnrick said, his voice easy, but there was an edge to it—a finality. "You got the first shot in over that bastard Lyle. Could've hesitated, could've let it drag out, but you didn't. A man like that don't waste time when it counts."

Harlan felt the words settle in his chest like a weight—not a burden, but something solid. Something real. He held McKinnrick's gaze, nodding once.

"Reckon he's as good a man as any to watch my back," McKinnrick finished, tipping the whiskey bottle in Harlan's direction before passing it along.

It hit Harlan in a way he hadn't expected. He'd ridden trails with other men, earned his pay on cattle drives, held his own when trouble found him, but this was different. It wasn't just a man's nod of respect after a job well done—it was something bigger. A place. A recognition.

He glanced around the fire, catching the expressions of the others. Dixon gave a slow nod, a sign of approval without words. Cutter, ever unreadable, and Poe grinned, tapping the butt of his revolver against his knee, but there was something in his eyes—maybe amusement, maybe something sharper.

It didn't matter. Harlan felt it. That weight shifting inside him. He wasn't just some hired gun passing through. He belonged here. McKinnrick didn't mention payment, but Harlan didn't need to ask. Good law work didn't come cheap.

The sun had barely climbed above the horizon when they set out, the morning air still holding a whisper of last night's chill. They rode hard, following the well-worn coach trail through dry country, the land stretched wide and empty, sagebrush and rock spilling out on either side.

Harlan kept his eyes ahead, watching the dust plume curling against the sky like a signal fire. The stage was moving steady, making good time, but they'd planned for that.

McKinnrick led them off the main trail well before the coach could spot them, guiding the group to a narrow pass where the road pinched tight between jagged rock formations. A perfect place to make sure a man couldn't run.

"Dixon, Cutter—you get high ground," McKinnrick ordered, pointing up toward the rocky outcrop. "Make sure that driver don't get brave."

The two men peeled off without a word, their rifles slung across their backs as they picked their way up the ridge.

Harlan sat still in the saddle as he and McKinnrick took up position in the open, their horses standing easy, like this was just another morning ride.

Harlan exhaled slow, shifting slightly in his saddle. His palm brushed over the worn handle of his Colt, a familiar weight, steady beneath his fingers. This was the part where everything could turn bad fast.

They didn't have to wait long.

The stage rounded the bend, the crack of the driver's whip carrying through the dry air, wheels rattling over uneven dirt. As soon as the coach came into view, the driver spotted them and pulled up hard, the horses rearing, snorting, throwing dust into the morning light. The passengers jolted forward as the wheels skidded, boots scraping against the wooden floorboards inside.

McKinnrick kept his posture easy, but his voice carried sharp and clear. "Ain't no need for anyone to get shot today." He lifted a hand, open-palmed, showing the driver he wasn't gunning just yet, and pulling his coat aside to show the badge. "We just need one man."

The driver swallowed, gripping the reins tight, eyes flicking toward Dixon and Cutter perched above. He knew there wasn't a way out of this, and his hands stayed steady on the lines, keeping the horses from bolting. The passengers—five of them—sat frozen in the coach, fear thick in the air. Harlan scanned the faces, looking for it—that shift, that flicker of recognition. Someone who already knew they were about to die.

And there he was.

Jed Royce.

Sitting near the front, gripping the bench seat hard enough that his knuckles turned white. His eyes darting left, right—looking for a way out.

Harlan felt it settle in his gut. The bastard knew he'd been caught. The moment stretched tight as a drawn wire. Dust swirled in the morning light, the scent of sweat and fear thick in the air.

Harlan didn't take his eyes off Jed Royce—the way his chest rose too fast, the slight twitch in his fingers like he was debating whether to go for iron.

McKinnrick moved first. Before Royce could think to run, McKinnrick grabbed a fistful of his coat and wrenched him off the stage. The man hit the dirt hard, tumbling over himself before landing on his back in the dust. The passengers inside the coach flinched, pressing back against their seats. One of them—a woman in a fine traveling dress—let out a sharp, startled gasp.

Royce coughed, rolled to his side, scrambling to his knees, palms sinking into the dirt. "You got the wrong man!" he spat, his voice raw with desperation. "I ain't done a damn thing!"

McKinnrick didn't hesitate. He reached into his coat and pulled out a folded piece of paper—a wanted poster. He dropped from the saddle and unfolding it slow, he stepped closer, holding the paper up beside Royce's dirt-streaked face. The likeness was near perfect. The strong jaw, the lean features, the scar running down from his right temple. Even with the dust on his skin, Royce was a dead match.

"Seems to me," McKinnrick said, voice calm, "you look a hell of a lot like this fella."

Royce lunged—not for a gun, just to move, just to get up.

He didn't make it far.

A rifle cracked.

The shot slammed into the dirt by his boot, sending up a spray of dust and rock. Royce froze mid-motion, his breathing ragged.

Dixon lowered his rifle from his perch on the ridge, smirking. "I'd sit still if I were you, friend."

Royce turned wide, panicked eyes back to McKinnrick. "You can't do this. Ain't no trial, no judge, no—"

McKinnrick didn't let him finish. His Colt cleared leather in one smooth motion—the barrel leveled steady, unwavering. One shot. The sound cracked through the canyon, sharp and final. Royce's body jerked back. A neat hole between his eyes. Then he was nothing but dead weight in the dust.

The passengers gasped, the woman inside the stage let out a sharp scream, pressing her hands to her mouth. The driver exhaled slow, turning his head away. Not his business. He'd seen worse.

Harlan didn't flinch.

Royce was wanted dead.

They'd done their job.

The smell of blood and gunpowder still lingered in the air as Dixon crouched by Royce's body, wiping the sweat from his brow.

"Get his arms," McKinnrick ordered.

Dixon didn't hesitate, grabbing Royce by the wrist and hauling him up. The corpse flopped like a rag doll, dust clinging to the fresh blood that seeped from the hole between his eyes. Harlan watched as Dixon slung the body over the back of his horse, tying him down like a sack of grain.

That should've been the end of it. But something caught Harlan's eye. A slight movement.

Poe.

He stood just near the open door of the stage, his broad frame partially blocking the view. But Harlan saw enough.

Poe's hand was out, palm open. His lips moved, speaking low and fast.

The old man he was talking to—a wiry, sun-beaten traveler clutching a battered carpetbag—was shaking. His fingers trembled as he dug into his pockets, pulled something free, and pressed it into Poe's hand. A woman beside him sat stiff, her knuckles white against the small coin purse she held tight in her lap, as Harlan watched Poe took it from her.

Harlan frowned.

It wasn't obvious. Wasn't a scene. No raised voices. No threats. Just a quiet exchange.A subtle demand. Poe turned, tucking whatever he'd taken into his coat as he stepped away from the stage like nothing had happened.

Harlan blinked, shaking the thought away.

Maybe he imagined it. Or maybe...Maybe McKinnrick lets Poe get away with a little. Harlan clenched his jaw, glancing toward McKinnrick, who was finishing up with the driver.

If he had seen it, he sure as hell didn't care.

Dixon swung into the saddle, Royce's body hanging limp behind him.

"Let's move," McKinnrick said, dusting his coat off.

Harlan took one last look at the stage. At the passengers, silent, staring. Then he turned away and rode after the gang.

The ride back was slow, the heat pressing down heavy, the dust thick in the air. Royce's body bounced lifelessly against Dixon's saddle, arms dangling, head lolling with each step of the horse. The blood had long since dried, turning black against the torn fabric of his shirt. No one spoke much. No need to.

Perdition Wells rose in the distance, its squat wooden buildings throwing long shadows in the afternoon light. The few townsfolk still lingering on the main street stopped what they were doing as the gang rode in, their eyes flicking to the dead man slumped over Dixon's saddle.

No one gasped. No one screamed.

This was the way things were.

McKinnrick rode straight to the sheriff's office, pulling up in front of the hitching post. The sheriff was already waiting, arms crossed over his chest, his expression unreadable. He was a broad man, thick around the middle, the kind who had likely been quick with his fists once but now settled disputes with a look and a hand near his gun belt. His eyes swept over the body, then up at McKinnrick.

"Royce?"

McKinnrick nodded. "Didn't give us much choice."

Sherrif Danvers exhaled slow, rubbing at the stubble on his jaw. "Ain't surprised." He turned, stepping back inside for a moment before returning with a small pouch of coins. He tossed it toward McKinnrick, who caught it without ceremony. There was a wanted poster with Royce's face on it, the sherrif tore it from the wall where it was pinned. Had McKiddrick just collected on Royce?

Dixon dragged Royce's body down from the saddle, letting it thump hard onto the ground. The sheriff motioned for his deputy, a younger man with a wary look, to come haul it out of the street. No one offered to help. No one cared much either way.

McKinnrick untied the pouch, weighing it in his palm before loosening the drawstring and shaking out a few coins into his hand. He counted quick, splitting the money, tossing silver into waiting palms.

Dixon first.

Poe next.

Then Cutter.

Then Harlan.

Harlan caught the coins and curled his fingers around it without hesitation. The silver was warm from the sun, heavy in his palm. Royce was guilty. That was all that mattered.

McKinnrick shared the money with the rest of the men then tucked the rest of the pouch into his coat and glanced around at them. "Drinks are on me tonight."

Dixon let out a low chuckle, flipping his coin before pocketing it. "That's a hell of a thing to hear."

Poe grinned, already stepping toward the saloon. Cutter followed, his expression unreadable as always.

Harlan stood for a second longer, watching the sheriff's deputy haul Royce's body away. The saloon doors banged once, and the voices of his crew faded into the warm, whiskey-scented air of the evening.

And then he shook it off.

The thing he thought he saw—the old man's trembling hands, the woman clutching her purse too tight, Poe leaning just a little too close—he shoved it down.

McKinnrick hadn't seen it. Or maybe he had and didn't care. But what did it matter? Harlan took a breath and followed the others inside.

CHAPTER 7: THE ILLUSION OF JUSTICE

The sun was just beginning to sink toward the western horizon, casting long, slow-moving shadows across the scrubland. The dust from their horses drifted behind them in the dry heat, curling up in the fading light like the last breath of a dying fire. It was quiet country out here. Open, empty, the kind of land where a man could disappear if he wanted to.

Harlan rode alongside McKinnrick, the rest of the gang spread out behind them. They had been riding most of the afternoon, following a lead on a gang of stagecoach robbers who'd been picking off supply runs between mining towns. McKinnrick had told them it was business—"We find 'em, put 'em down, and get paid for the trouble." Seemed fair enough.

Harlan had done work like this before—riding protection for cattle drives, keeping men honest with a gun. But this was different. This felt like something more.

McKinnrick rode easy in the saddle, like he was built for it, his coat pushed back just enough to show the holster slung low at his hip. The man carried himself like someone who had nothing to prove—just a quiet certainty that the world would move around him if he willed it to.

After a while, he broke the silence.

"You ever think about what it takes to keep a place standing?" McKinnrick asked, his voice even, his eyes ahead on the trail.

Harlan glanced over. "What do you mean?"

McKinnrick gave a small nod toward the open country ahead. "You ever wonder why some towns last and others don't?" He shifted in the saddle, rolling his shoulders. "Ain't the soil. Ain't the buildings. Ain't even the people, most times."

Harlan waited.

McKinnrick sighed, rubbing a hand across his jaw before continuing. "A town lasts because someone holds the line. Because someone's willing to do the dirty work." His voice lowered slightly. "That's what I do, Harlan. That's what we do. We hold the line. We make sure men like those sons of bitches we're trackin' don't tear things apart."

Harlan frowned slightly, thinking on it. McKinnrick wasn't wrong. He had seen it plenty—towns eaten up by gangs, ranchers bled dry by rustlers, lawmen too weak or too crooked to stop it. Maybe McKinnrick really was different. Maybe this wasn't just another gang pretending at law.

McKinnrick exhaled, adjusting his reins slightly. "I rode with the Rangers before the war."

Harlan blinked. That was the first time McKinnrick had ever mentioned anything about his past. "That so?" he asked.

McKinnrick gave a small nod. "Yeah. Spent years chasing men like the ones we're after now. Hard men. Mean sons of bitches. Some of 'em did it 'cause they liked killin'. Others did it 'cause they didn't know how to live any other way. We put 'em in the ground just the same." He was quiet for a long moment after that, watching the horizon. Then, in a lower voice, he said, "Saw a lot of good men die. Too many."

Harlan didn't press him. Didn't ask what had happened, why he'd left. Didn't need to. A man didn't talk about the things that had broken him.

McKinnrick turned toward Harlan then, his expression unreadable. "Ain't much law left in the world, but I do what I can to keep order where I ride."

Harlan studied him for a second, trying to find the lie. He didn't see one. Instead, he saw a man who spoke with conviction, who believed what he was saying.

The wind had died by the time they reached the cave system, leaving the land silent, heavy with the weight of something coming. The moon sat high, spilling pale light over the jagged ridgeline, making the rock formations look like petrified ghosts, twisted and waiting.

McKinnrick pulled up first, lifting a hand for the rest of them to halt. Harlan reined in alongside him, eyes scanning the dark mouth of the cave ahead. It was cut into the side of a low hill, barely more than a black gash in the rock, but it would be hell to root men out of it if they were dug in deep.

McKinnrick turned in his saddle, speaking low. "Dixon, Poe—take the back way in. Cut off their escape. Harlan, you ride with me. We go in fast, keep 'em pinned down."

There were no arguments. The men moved easy, splitting off in silence. They had done this before. Harlan's grip tightened on his Colt. So had he.

They dismounted just beyond the treeline and crept forward on foot. McKinnrick moved like a man who had done this too many times to count, his revolver loose in his grip, his steps quiet against the dirt. Harlan followed just behind him, his boots scuffing over loose rock. The entrance was wide but low, the ceiling sloping down into blackness. Inside, a faint glow flickered—a fire burning somewhere deeper in the cavern.

McKinnrick crouched low beside the rock, tilted his head, listening. A voice carried from within, rough, laughing. They weren't expecting trouble. McKinnrick gave a slow nod. Then he moved.

The first gunshot shattered the silence.

A man stumbled out of the firelight, a pistol barely clearing his holster before McKinnrick put a round through his chest.

Harlan followed him in, gun leveled, his boots kicking up dust as he moved through the cavern.

Chaos.

The outlaws scrambled for their guns, knocking over crates, cursing as they tripped over each other in the narrow space. One of them—a wiry bastard with a scraggly mustache—managed to raise a shotgun.

Harlan didn't hesitate.

He fired once, the shot slamming into the man's gut, folding him over like he'd been struck with a hammer. He went down hard, knocking over the fire in the process, sending embers skittering across the dirt.

A second outlaw bolted for the exit.

He didn't get far. A gunshot cracked from outside—Poe or Dixon laying him down before he reached daylight.

The last one—a kid, no older than twenty, hands shaking as he backed up against the cave wall—dropped his gun before he even had the chance to use it.

"Please—" His voice was ragged, desperate. "I give up, I swear to God, I give up!"

Harlan's breath was coming quick, gun still raised, his heart hammering from the fight. He saw McKinnrick step forward, saw his fingers tighten on the grip of his Colt. For a second, Harlan thought he was going to do it—put a bullet in the kid's head, right then and there.

But McKinnrick just exhaled slow. "Get on your knees."

The outlaw hesitated, but one look in McKinnrick's eyes made him obey. Hands in the dirt, head down, mouth shut.

McKinnrick holstered his gun, turning back to his men. "Tie 'em up," he said, voice cool, steady. "We'll take 'em back to town."

Harlan stood there for a moment, gun still clutched in his grip, and nodded at McKinnrick.

The town came alive when they rode in, lanterns flickering to life, doors swinging open, voices rising in murmured excitement.

The sheriff met them in the street, stepping out of his office, a few nervous deputies at his side. He took one look at the outlaws, their hands bound, bloodied but alive, and let out a relieved breath. "Damn good work," he muttered.

The mayor appeared next, an older man with a worried face that eased into relief when he saw McKinnrick. "You did what you promised," he said, offering his hand.

McKinnrick shook it, calm, unbothered. "Always do."

The mayor handed him a small leather pouch, the clink of coins audible inside. McKinnrick took it without even glancing down, stuffing it into his coat.

"Sheriff," he said, turning back, "I suggest you hang the ones that need hangin'."

The sheriff gave a short nod, no protest. Like McKinnrick was the law. And for the first time since he started riding with him, Harlan believed it.

That night, around the table in the saloon McKinnrick leaned forward slightly, elbows on the table, the lamplight flickering in his sharp, knowing eyes. "I don't pretend to be some saint," he said, voice easy, but with that edge of finality. "But there's a right way and a wrong way to do things. And I don't much care for men who take without paying their dues."

Harlan nodded, rolling the words over in his head. He'd spent a long time drifting, taking whatever came, never knowing where he fit in. But now? Maybe he'd found a man worth following.

The saloon was alive with the kind of reckless energy that only comes after a victory. The piano clanged in the corner, barely keeping up with the drunken chatter and laughter bouncing off the walls. Lantern light flickered in the smoky air, catching the glint of whiskey bottles and silver coins tumbling across the poker table.

McKinnrick's men had taken over the place, drinking deep, their voices loud with satisfaction. They'd earned their pay today—and tonight was for spending it.

Harlan sat at the bar, a whiskey glass in his hand, the warmth of it settling low in his chest. He was relaxed in a way he hadn't been in a long time. The job had been clean. No senseless bloodshed, no shakedowns, no looking over his shoulder. Just riding the trail, hunting down bad men, bringing them to justice.

A familiar voice broke through the hum of the saloon. "Drink up, Harlan."

He turned as McKinnrick stepped up beside him, rolling a silver coin across his knuckles before flicking it onto the bar. A signal for another round.

The barkeep slid fresh drinks their way, and McKinnrick lifted his glass.

"Hell of a job today." His eyes gleamed with approval. "You handled yourself like a man who knows what he's doing."

Harlan smirked. "Guess I ain't new to this kind of work."

McKinnrick clinked his glass against Harlan's. "Ain't about being new. It's about knowing which way to point your iron and when to pull the trigger." He took a slow sip, savoring it. "You got that instinct. Saw it when you shot Lyle. Most men don't."

Harlan felt a flicker of something—pride, maybe. It had been a long time since anyone had spoken to him like he was worth something.

McKinnrick leaned against the bar, casting a glance around the saloon. "Towns like this—weak law, folks too scared to stand up for themselves—they get swallowed up if a man don't hold the line.

He exhaled, swirling the whiskey in his glass. "That's what we do, Harlan. We keep the peace. And we get paid for it."

Harlan let the words settle. It made sense. Maybe he'd spent too much time drifting, working cattle drives, keeping to himself, wondering what the hell he was supposed to do with his life. Maybe all he needed was the right cause. The right man to follow.

McKinnrick smirked, tilting his glass toward him. "You're one of us now. Ain't just some hired hand. You ride with me, you ain't just working a job—you're part of something bigger."

Harlan lifted his glass, feeling the weight of those words settle deep in his gut. One of us. He hadn't belonged anywhere in a long time.

It felt good.

McKinnrick nodded to him, then turned, slipping back into the revelry of the saloon, laughing at something Dixon said, clapping Poe on the back. Harlan stayed at the bar a little longer, finishing his drink slow, letting the feeling linger. Tonight, he wasn't an outlaw. He wasn't a drifter. For the first time in a long while, he didn't feel restless. He felt like he was exactly where he was supposed to be. Harlan crossed the room and joined the poker game.

The saloon was busier than the town deserved, filled with the sound of dice rattling, whiskey being poured, and boots scuffing against the floorboards. The oil lamps burned low, casting long shadows over the faces of men fresh off a kill, fresh off a job that had them drinking easier and laughing louder. Harlan sat at a table near the back, watching his cards, watching the men around him, and watching the woman who had caught his attention.

She had been moving through the saloon all night, a slim thing with dark hair falling loose around her shoulders, eyes that had seen plenty but still held enough light to draw a man in. She worked the room like she owned it, laughing at whispered promises, pressing herself against men when they had the coin, but she hadn't left with anyone yet.

Not yet.

Harlan took another drink, a slow pull of whiskey, feeling it burn in his throat. The night had been good to him. He had money in his pocket, still warm from the mayor's hand. His boots were dusted, his belly full, and the ache in his bones wasn't from hunger or wounds—it was the kind of tired that came after a job well done. He was ready for the night to end in a woman's arms.

When the card game broke, Harlan stood, rolling his shoulders, tossing back the last of his drink. He caught her eye across the room and tipped his head, signaling. She gave him a look—long enough to make him think she'd follow—then she smirked and shook her head.

"Waitin' on your boss," she said, voice honeyed but firm.

Harlan stiffened just a little, but he kept his face easy. He stepped closer, letting his hands rest loose at his sides. "There's plenty of women here," he said. "Ain't gonna miss you."

She tilted her head, amused, like she was weighing her options. Then she laughed softly, flicking her fingers against his coat. "You pay like him?"

Harlan grinned. "You come with me, you'll find out."

She hesitated, her eyes flicking toward the stairway, the rooms upstairs. Then she took his hand and led him up. The bed wasn't much, just a mattress on a wooden frame, the sheets clean enough. The lamp on the dresser flickered, throwing shadows that moved with them. She undressed slow, letting the fabric slide off her shoulders, watching him as he sat on the edge of the bed, undoing his gun belt, peeling off his coat.

She was young, soft where it mattered, sharp where it counted. She ran a hand over his chest, fingers trailing over old scars, nails grazing down his ribs, like she cared. And right now Harlan wanted someone to care, and tonight he was willing to fool himself into believing that she did.

The sound came from below in the saloon. A voice, cutting through the saloon like a blade. McKinnrick. The girl froze, her body going rigid at the sound below. Harlan heard it too, but he ignored it, sliding his arms around her waist.

She pushed at his chest, tension in her limbs. "Damn it," she hissed. "I gotta go. Son of a bitch," she muttered, yanking the dress back over her head and snatching up her boots.

Harlan just stood there for a second, breathing deep, feeling the sweat cooling between them, watching her move frantic in the dim light.

Then she was gone, slipping out the door without a backward glance.

McCoy's Last Bet

By the time Harlan stepped out of the saloon the next morning, the town was waking slow. The dust was already kicking up in the street, the heat rising in waves off the rooftops. He adjusted his hat, his belt, and moved toward his horse. That's when he saw her.

She stood near the saloon entrance, leaning against the post, her arms folded, a hard scowl fixed to her face. And her right eye was blackened. Harlan felt a slow burn creep up his spine. She just spat into the dirt, turned her head, and disappeared inside. Harlan exhaled, stepped into the stirrup, and swung into the saddle. As he rode out, he didn't look back.

CHAPTER 8: CRACKS IN THE LAW

The wind carried the dry scent of cattle and dust as the gang rode toward the run-down spread that passed for a ranch. The buildings were weathered, the fencing barely holding, and the cattle too thin from the summer heat. Nothing about the place looked like it could house a dangerous outlaw. But McKinnrick had been certain.

James Calder. Ex-convict. Rustler. Killer.

Harlan had learned not to question McKinnrick's instincts. If he said Calder was here, then he was here.

The group pulled up near the main barn, their horses kicking up clouds of dust. A man stepped out onto the porch of the ranch house, a gray-haired rancher, his shoulders squared but his expression wary as he took them in. His hands stayed visible, nowhere near the old revolver that hung from his hip, but his eyes flicked from face to face, measuring.

McKinnrick rode forward slow, tipping his hat. "You the owner here?"

The rancher nodded. "Nathan Boone."

McKinnrick gave a slow, knowing smile. "We're looking for a man. James Calder."

A beat. Something shifted in Boone's face. Just a flicker, but Harlan caught it.

"Don't know him," Boone said, too quick.

McKinnrick's smile didn't falter, but something in his posture changed—just enough to make the air heavier. "That so?"

Boone's jaw tensed. "I got a handful of men working for me. Some come and go. But I ain't harboring no outlaws."

McKinnrick didn't break his gaze.

Then Dixon spoke up, his voice carrying. "Funny, 'cause we heard different."

Behind Boone, the barn doors creaked open. A man stepped out, wiping his hands on a rag, his shoulders broad but hunched like he carried too much weight.

Calder.

He wasn't the bloodthirsty killer McKinnrick had made him out to be. He looked like any other ranch hand—weathered, tired, just trying to make it to the next day. When he saw them, he froze. Harlan watched his hand drift toward his hip, hesitation in his every move.

Boone stepped in front of him. "Hold on now," he said, his voice steady but edged with something close to fear. "Whatever you're here for, I think you got it wrong. Calder's been working for me six months. He's done good work, kept his nose clean."

McKinnrick's face stayed unreadable. "That so?"

Boone nodded. "The charges against him— they ain't what you think. He was a kid when he got locked up. Wrong place, wrong time. He's got a past, sure, but he's been trying to live straight."

McKinnrick said nothing. Just sat there, watching Calder. The tension stretched. Harlan felt it coming before it happened.

McKinnrick drew and fired.

The gunshot cracked through the air. Calder jerked back, a red bloom spreading across his chest as he staggered, eyes wide, hands grasping at nothing. He hit the dirt hard.

Boone swore, dropping to his knees beside the dying man. "Goddamn you," he hissed, his voice rough, grief and fury mixing as he grabbed Calder's still-warm body.

McKinnrick holstered his gun, his face unreadable. Harlan swallowed, his grip tightening on the reins.

McKinnrick exhaled slow, adjusting his coat, then turned back toward the men. "Get the receipt."

Dixon moved first, rolling his shoulders before stepping toward the body, "Hey, Harlan, give me hand."

Harlan followed slower.

Calder lay face-down in the dirt, his blood mixing with the dust, turning it into something dark and thick. His arms were twisted under him, his hat knocked loose a few feet away, the wind picking at the brim.

Harlan crouched down, gripping Calder's shoulder and rolling him over. His head lolled, the wound at his chest a neat, final thing. The man had the calloused hands of a ranch worker, fingers rough, nails chipped and worn from roping branding, and fence-mending. His skin was sunburnt, the deep kind that didn't fade, just layered over itself season after season, marking him as a man who had worked outside his whole life. Boone was right. He'd been a ranch hand. Not a killer. Not a bandit. Just a man trying to outrun something he couldn't.

Harlan swallowed, jaw tightening. Boone still stood off to the side, his face carved from something hard, something beyond grief.

Dixon didn't hesitate. He grabbed Calder's arms while Harlan took his legs, and together, they hauled him up, hoisting him over the back of a waiting horse. Calder's body flopped like a rag doll, the weight of him shifting as the saddle creaked. Dixon worked quick, tying the body down like just another piece of cargo—one more thing to be delivered to the Sheriff.

McKinnrick dusted off his gloves. He didn't even look at Calder. Didn't look at Boone, either. Just turned to the men.

"Mount up."

Then Boone finally spoke, his voice quiet but sharp. "He didn't deserve that."

McKinnrick paused and looked back. Smirked. "Deserve ain't got nothin' to do with it." Then he kicked his horse forward, leading them out.

They rode into town just as the sun sank low, the sky painted in streaks of gold and red, the kind of colors that made a man think of fire and dying light. The dust clung to them, their horses moving at a steady lope, the weight of the body bouncing lifelessly against Dixon's saddle.

Calder had been dead for hours now, but that didn't seem to matter much.

The people of Perdition Wells watched them as they passed, but no one said a word. A few turned their heads, some ducked inside buildings, doors shutting with quiet finality. No one asked what happened. No one needed to.

Harlan rode near the back, watching as McKinnrick led them straight to the Sheriff's office, the same way a man might lead a packhorse carrying freight.

When they pulled up outside, the Sheriff was already waiting. He was an older man, built thick around the shoulders, the weight of his badge sitting heavier on him than the iron at his hip. He took one long look at Calder's body, still tied across the horse, and let out a slow breath through his nose.

"That him?"

McKinnrick swung down from the saddle, dusting off his coat and smiling. "Sure is, Sherrif O'Dell."

O'Dell stepped forward, gripping the back of Calder's shirt and hauling him over onto the dirt like a sack of grain. The dead man hit the ground with a dull thud, his body folding in on itself, face half-buried in the dust.

O'Dell crouched, studied the wound, then nodded. "Yeah. That's him." He stood, straightened his belt, then turned toward his deputy, a wiry kid who looked like he had too much conscience for this line of work.

"Go fetch Antrim and his boys and him in the ground," the sheriff said to the deputy. The deputy swallowed hard, hesitating, but O'Dell didn't wait for him to move. Instead, he walked back inside, leaving Calder where he lay.

McKinnrick followed.

Harlan took his time dismounting, trailing in behind the others. The inside of the Sheriff's office smelled of sweat, old leather, and the faintest trace of whiskey. A wanted board hung against the wall, names and faces of men who wouldn't see the next year.

O'Dell stepped behind his desk, opened a wooden drawer, and pulled out a leather pouch heavy with silver.

He tossed it onto the desk with a dull *thump.*

McKinnrick picked it up without hesitation, untying the string and checking the weight in his palm. He counted quickly and smoothly, like a man used to handling this kind of transaction.

Satisfied, he slid the coins into his coat pocket.

Harlan felt the weight settle in his gut. This wasn't law. This was blood money.

The Sherrif leaned back in his chair, rubbing at the graying stubble on his chin. "I appreciate you bringing him in."

McKinnrick gave that slow, easy smirk. "Always happy to serve."

O'Dell nodded, then gestured toward the door. That was it. No thanks, no condolences, just another deal done.

When they stepped outside, McKinnrick loosened the pouch, splitting the bounty the way he always did. Dixon, Poe, Cutter, and the rest—each took their cut with no hesitation.

McKinnrick handed Harlan his share. Harlan looked at it for a long moment, the silver coins catching the last of the dying light. He reached out and took them. Because what else was he supposed to do? Calder was guilty. That's what he told himself. That's all that mattered.

But as he shoved the money into his coat, he couldn't shake the feeling that this was different.

And for the first time, Harlan saw McKinnrick for what he really was.

Not a lawman.

Not a man serving justice.

Just another outlaw, a bounty hunter with a stolen badge.

Harlon rode near the back of the group, letting the others pull ahead. His mouth was dry, and the taste of road dust and something else was sitting bitter on his tongue.

Something in him had turned over when Calder fell.

He'd been riding with McKinnrick long enough to know how things worked, how men sometimes didn't get second chances. He'd seen plenty of killings and had done his fair share. But something about this one gnawed at him, made his stomach twist in a way he didn't like. Calder hadn't drawn a gun before McKinnrick cut him down. Didn't matter that Boone swore the man was trying to live straight. Didn't matter that he might've had something to say before McKinnrick took the chance away.

The law was supposed to ask questions. But McKinnrick didn't ask. He just shot.

Harlon let his horse slow as they approached a creek, the others riding ahead, their voices carrying but distant. He leaned forward, giving his mount its head, letting it drink deep from the cool water.

The fire burned low, orange embers glowing in the pit as the whiskey bottle passed from hand to hand. The night was quiet, save for the crackle of burning wood and the occasional murmur of laughter from the men stretched around the fire. Harlan sat a little ways off, nursing his drink, his back resting against the trunk of a gnarled mesquite tree.

He could see McKinnrick clear as day, leaning back on his saddle, one boot crossed over the other, telling some story about chasing Apaches through the Rio Grande country. The men listened, laughing at the right parts, hanging on his every word like he was a damn folk hero.

Harlan didn't laugh.

Didn't smile.

Just watched.

The whiskey in his tin cup tasted bitter, or maybe that was just his mood. His eyes trailed over McKinnrick's face, the easy confidence in his posture, the way he told a tale like he'd lived a hundred lives and seen more than any man should. Harlan had believed it, too, once. Believed McKinnrick was something close to a lawman, that they were out here doing the right kind of work— hunting men who needed hunting, bringing justice where the law couldn't reach.

But he'd seen too much now.

And now, sitting here, watching McKinnrick hold court around the fire, whiskey sloshing in his hand, grinning like he owned the world, Harlan couldn't shake the cold weight settling in his gut.

How many times had this played out before? How many men had McKinnrick dragged to the dirt under the banner of the law, only to make a deal with the highest bidder once the dust settled? He'd called Calder's body a receipt – that had sickened Harlan to the core.

Cutter sat nearby, hands resting loosely on his knees. Dixon and Poe were still laughing, still riding the high of an easy kill and a job well done. They didn't see it. Didn't want to. Or maybe they'd known all along and just didn't care.

Harlan drained the last of his whiskey and let the tin cup dangle from his fingers. His pulse was steady and slow, but there was a different kind of fire burning in his chest now.

He wasn't stupid.

He wasn't about to start mouthing off, calling McKinnrick out in front of his own men. That was a fast way to get himself shot and left for the coyotes.

But the shine was wearing off.

The man he thought he was following—the man he thought he was learning from—wasn't who he'd seemed to be. And the longer Harlan rode with him, the more it felt like he was riding toward something he wouldn't be able to come back from. He sat there in the flickering firelight, listening to the laughter, feeling the whiskey warm his throat, and told himself one thing.

This doesn't end the way I thought it would.

And deep down, he already knew it wasn't gonna end well.

CHAPTER 7: A BAD FEELING GETS WORSE

By the time they reached Benton Creek, the heat had settled heavy on their backs. The sky had gone pale with midday, the air thick with dust that rose in slow, choking waves beneath the horses' hooves. The town was small and tired, the kind of place that barely held together, patched up by whatever its people could scavenge or spare. A few crooked ranch houses, a lean-to stable, a saloon with its sign half-falling from rusted chains. And in the center of it all, like a heartbeat trying to keep time, the general store.

McKinnrick led the way, riding straight into the main street like he owned the ground beneath him. His stallion moved smooth and unhurried, his coat dust-streaked but fine, his revolver riding easy on his hip. Behind him, his men fanned out, spreading through the town in a slow, deliberate wave. Not reckless. Not loud. Just making themselves known. Harlan hung back, letting his buckskin keep pace at the rear. Watching.

It didn't take long to see it. The people of Benton Creek reacted the same way every man and woman did when the law came riding into town. Except this wasn't the law, And the fear was different. A woman dragged her child back into a doorway, her hands tight on his shoulders. A rancher standing near the hitching post lowered his head, his fingers curling around the brim of his hat like he was debating whether to tip it or just disappear altogether. A saloon girl peered from behind a lace curtain, her fingers gripping the edge just enough to see before she let the fabric drop, her shadow retreating into the dim light.

Harlan felt it then—the thing he'd been suspecting since he first rode with McKinnrick. They didn't look at him like he was a hero. They didn't look at him like he was a savior. They looked at him like a man they owed something to. This was a town that wasn't pleased to see McKinnrick. McKinnrick dismounted with the slow confidence of a man who expected no trouble. He dusted off his coat and took his time tying his reins to the post outside the general store.

The store owner. A tall, wiry man, skin weathered and drawn tight from too many years under the sun. He wore an apron streaked with flour and sweat, his hands wringing together before he had the sense to stop them. McKinnrick stepped inside, Harlan behind him, and the owner followed. The room was dim and cluttered, the shelves lined with sacks of grain, bolts of cloth, crates of canned goods. The place smelled of old wood and dust, the floor worn thin in front of the counter where men had stood for years, handing over whatever money.

The store owner tried to straighten his shoulders, but Harlan saw the truth of him—his back was already bent. McKinnrick didn't say anything right away. Just let the silence settle, thick and unmoving. Then slowly, he said. "Good to see you, Cartright."

Cartwright swallowed hard. "Wasn't expectin' you this early, McKinnrick."

McKinnrick gave a slow, polite nod. "I like to keep folks on their toes."

Cartwright's Adam's apple bobbed. His hands clenched together again before he forced them to his sides.

McKinnrick leaned on the counter. "You got it?"

Cartwright hesitated. Just for a second. McKinnrick didn't move. Didn't change expression. But that second lasted too long. Cartwright exhaled sharply, reached beneath the counter, and pulled out a battered envelope, setting it down in front of McKinnrick like a man making an offering. McKinnrick flipped it open, reviewed the contents, and slid it inside his coat. Cartwright watched him close, his fingers twitching against the counter. Sweat gathered at his brow, his breath coming a little too quick.

"Things have been slow," Cartwright said, his voice strained. "Railroad's pulled most of the work outta here. Cattle runs ain't what they used to be. If you could just—"

McKinnrick raised a hand. Not fast. Not aggressive. Just enough to make Cartwright stop talking. "You've done your part, Cartwright. No need to whine about it."

Cartwright's mouth snapped shut.

McKinnrick smiled. "Pleasure doin' business."

Harlan watched the way Cartwright exhaled when McKinnrick's back was turned. Like a man who had just handed over a ransom. McKinnrick stepped off the boardwalk. He caught Harlan watching. For a second, nothing passed between them. Then McKinnrick smiled. "Ain't the law and order a beautiful thing?"

Harlan didn't answer.

The fire burned low, casting long shadows across the scrubland. The whiskey bottle had made its rounds, but Harlan hadn't taken much. He sat a little apart from the others, rolling a cigarette slow. McKinnrick sat near the flames, leaning back against his saddle, his hat tipped just enough to keep the firelight out of his eyes. Harlan struck a match, lit his cigarette, and exhaled slow. The night stretched wide and silent around them, the hills rolling dark beneath the open sky. The whiskey passed around enough times to loosen tongues and dull the edges of whatever guilt they might have carried.

But Harlan wasn't drinking tonight.

He sat apart from the others, rolling a cigarette slow, his mind circling the thing he'd seen earlier—the quiet exchange between McKinnrick and Cartwright.

He exhaled through his nose, flicking his eyes across the fire. Dixon and Poe were talking in low voices, grinning over some crude joke. The others were settling in, stretching out under their blankets, letting the night claim them.

Cutter sat a little apart and didn't look at him when he spoke. "Something on your mind, Harlan?"

The words were casual, almost lazy, but they landed too neat, too knowing. Harlan hesitated, staring at the ember at the tip of his cigarette. Then he shook his head.

Cutter smirked like he knew better. "That so?"

Harlan took another drag, then said. "Town didn't seem too pleased to see us."

Cutter smirked, adjusting his hat. "Nope. Don't reckon they were."

Harlan waited, but Cutter didn't offer more, so he pressed. "They in debt to McKinnrick?"

Cutter sighed, rubbing his jaw like he was considering how much to say. Finally, he turned his head slightly toward Harlan. "They weren't always like this. A few years back, Benton Creek was just another piss-stop on the cattle trails, but they had themselves a problem. Family by the name of Oakley."

Harlan frowned. "Ranchers?"

"More like thieves that owned the deed," Cutter said. "Had their hands in everything—store, saloon, freight wagons. They ran this place, bled it dry. Folks couldn't make a move without payin' for the privilege. You needed lumber? You bought it from the Oakley's. Needed a loan? You took it from them—and God help you if you were late."

Harlan exhaled slowly. "And McKinnrick got rid of them?"

Cutter grinned, slow and knowing. "Somethin' like that."

Harlan looked at him, waiting for more, but Cutter didn't reply. "Town must've been grateful," Harlan said.

Cutter gave a small shrug. "Sure. They were. But see, that's the thing. Law ain't free. Ain't like the state's sendin' deputies to places like this. Men like McKinnrick, we step in, we handle things, and we make sure everything stays quiet afterward."

Harlan nodded slowly. It made a kind of sense. "So they still owe him."

Cutter nodded. "They couldn't pay what they promised back then. So, every once in a while, we swing by. Make sure they remember the arrangement." He glanced at Harlan, grinning. "Call it an investment in their own safety."

Harlan thought about that. Thought about Cartwright's face, about the way the town had gone still when they rode in. Fear, yeah, but also something else. Resignation. Like they understood the cost of keeping the Oakleys gone.

Cutter clapped him on the shoulder, pushing away from the hitching post. "Don't let it keep you up, Harlan. Town's still standin'. People are still breathin'. That's worth somethin'."

Harlan nodded, taking one last pull from his cigarette before flicking it into the dust. Maybe Cutter was right. Maybe McKinnrick wasn't shaking them down—just collecting what he was owed. And wasn't that just the way of things? Law wasn't free. And neither was McKinnrick.

"Benton Creek ain't the only place that owes us," Cutter continued, his voice easy like they were just talking horses or the weather.

Harlan frowned. "No?"

Cutter shook his head, tucking his hands into his gun belt. "McKinnrick calls it 'doing the rounds.' We got a few places we keep an eye on. Towns that needed a hand and didn't have no law of their own, ranches that owe us."

Harlan exhaled slowly, glancing back toward the store, where Cartwright was no doubt counting up whatever was left after McKinnrick walked out with his share. "How many?"

Cutter shrugged. "Half a dozen, give or take. Some bigger, some smaller. All of 'em needed McKinnrick at one time or another."

Harlan thought on that. He knew what it was like, riding through towns with no sheriff, no law.

Cutter must've caught the hesitation on his face because he gave him a look, sharp and sure. "These towns would be dead if it wasn't for McKinnrick."

Harlan met his gaze.

Cutter tilted his head toward the storefront. "Cartwright might be sweating, but he's still got a store, don't he? Folks still got homes, still got cattle in the fields. No bandits runnin' off their stock, no gangs comin' through and taking what they please. We keep the peace. And sometimes, that peace costs a little extra."

Harlan let the words sit.

Cutter smirked and slapped him on the back. "Ain't nothin' to be bothered about."

Harlan gave a slow nod, but the feeling in his gut still hadn't settled.

CHAPTER 8: THE COST OF PROTECTION

The heat came early. The sky stretched out, dull and pale blue, without a single cloud to break up the glare. The sun had barely lifted over the jagged ridges in the east, but already the air was warming, the dry wind pulling moisture from the land before it had the chance to settle. The desert wasn't awake yet, but it was stirring, the first hints of shimmering heat waves rising off the cracked earth.

They rode in a loose line, hooves kicking up dust that stuck to their sweat-dampened clothes. The land stretched endless before them—rolling scrub, sunbaked rock, dry washes where nothing but ghosts of old rivers remained. The only sound was the slow creak of leather, the occasional snort of a horse, and the murmured voices of McKinnrick's men. Harlan rode near the back, his buckskin moving smooth beneath him.

Poe spat into the dirt, a wet thud against the dry, cracked earth, then wiped his mouth with the back of his hand. His grin was too wide, too sharp—like a man already enjoying a joke that hadn't been told yet. "Think ol' Tate is feelin' charitable today?"

Beside him, Dixon chuckled, adjusting his grip on the reins. His broad shoulders shifted beneath his dust-coated coat, his rifle resting easy in the saddle holster. "Man ain't got much choice but to be."

A few of the others laughed. Not big belly laughs, not forced, uneasy chuckles. Just the quiet amusement of men who knew exactly what kind of day this was going to be.

Harlan didn't laugh. Instead, he felt his gut tighten, slow and steady, like a coil winding itself up.

McKinnrick rode at the head, tall in the saddle, his stallion cutting an easy path across the dusty terrain. His coat flared slightly when the wind picked up, the dust collecting on his boots and the hem of his duster, but he didn't seem to notice. Or maybe he just didn't care. Harlan watched him close. McKinnrick never looked back. Never needed to. The men followed him without hesitation, without question. That kind of loyalty didn't come easy. Didn't come cheap, either.

The land began to shift. The flat, open desert gave way to rolling hills, a few low, craggy ridges jutting out like the ribs of some long-dead beast. A dried-out creek bed wound through the valley, the remains of old water long since gone. And then, finally, Harrison Fork came into view.

It wasn't much. Just a handful of ranch houses, a general store, a saloon with a sagging roof, and a blacksmith's shop that looked half-collapsed on itself. Another town on its last legs. But the people were still trying. Harlan could see it in the neatly patched fences, the wagon tracks worn deep into the dirt from supply runs, the lines of drying clothes strung between homes, catching the wind like tired flags. These were hard people. The kind that didn't break easy. But Harlan knew better than most—a man didn't have to break to be forced to bend.

Near the hitching post, a rancher stopped mid-motion, his hand halfway to his horse's bridle. His shoulders tensed, his head lowering slightly. He didn't move. Didn't turn. Just stood there, staring at the ground. Harlan felt it then like a slow, creeping thing settling into the dirt beneath them.

McKinnrick swung down from his horse, dusted off his coat, and tied his reins slow, deliberate. He stretched, rolling his shoulders like a man shaking off the weight of the ride, then turned to the others with a smirk. "Who wants a drink, boys?"

A few grins cracked across dust-covered faces. Dixon spat into the dirt, Poe ran a hand over his jaw.

They moved toward the saloon, boots clunking heavy on the boardwalk. The town watched but didn't linger—folks turned their heads and kept moving, doors shutting soft but firm as they passed.

The barkeep was stood behind the bar when they walked in. He wasn't a man who smiled much, and he sure as hell wasn't smiling now. The apron around his waist was stained with whiskey and grease, his sleeves rolled to the elbow, showing thin, wiry arms that looked like they once held more strength than they did now.

McKinnrick walked up slow, planting both hands on the counter. He didn't say a word; he didn't need to.

The barkeep swallowed once, then wordlessly reached for a bottle; he lined up the glasses without being asked, pouring quick, his hands steady but his jaw tight.

McKinnrick watched him as he poured, then smiling, said. "Thank you, Tate."

When Tate finished, McKinnrick picked up his glass and lifted it in a silent toast to his men. "To a job well done."

The others took glasses and drank.

Tate didn't.

He just stood there, watching the level in the bottle drop, waiting for whatever was coming next. The moment stretched. A silent conversation passed between them.

"You got it?" McKinnrick asked, setting down his empty whiskey glass.

Tate's fingers twitched just barely. Without a word, he reached into his apron, pulled out a small leather pouch, opened it, slewed out the contents into his palm, and handed over most of it. His movements were tight, forced—like every part of him was resisting.

McKittrick took it and weighed it in his palm, and his eyes scanned the coins for a moment, counting them before they disappeared inside his coat. Then McKinnrick smiled. "Good man." He leaned across the bar and clapped Tate on the shoulder.

Tate didn't flinch. But Harlan saw it—the way the man's jaw clenched, the way his shoulders stiffened. The anger in his eyes.

This wasn't business.

This wasn't law.

This was extortion.

And Harlan had just helped collect.

They'd left Harrison Fork behind, but its weight still clung to Harlan's skin. The uneasy silence of the townsfolk, the way they'd stepped aside, the way Tate had handed over his earnings with a clenched jaw and a hollow look—it all sat in Harlan's gut like a stone that wouldn't pass.

Dixon rode up alongside McKinnrick, chewing on a strip of jerky, his mouth twisting around the dried meat as he spoke.

"What about Morrissey?"

McKinnrick's stallion flicked its ears back, but McKinnrick himself didn't shift. "What about him?"

Dixon shrugged. "Been slow, same as Tate. Claimed his herd took a bad hit. Said he'd have it next time."

A beat passed.

Then McKinnrick exhaled slowly, adjusting his gloves. "Let's pay him a visit."

The Morrissey homestead sat low against the earth, a single cabin, a barn with sagging beams, a corral with only a handful of half-starved cattle picking through brittle grass. There was no sign of extra hands, no movement save for a lone horse tied off at the post outside the cabin. A man stood on the porch, arms crossed, watching them ride in.

Thomas Morrissey.

Broad, sunburned, built by hard labor and long days. His shirt was damp with sweat, his boots were worn but sturdy, and his hands were rough as cut stone. A rifle leaned against the doorframe, not far from his reach, but he didn't make a move for it.

Didn't have to.

He knew it was already too late for that.

McKinnrick's men fanned out, taking their time, their horses shifting beneath them, hooves stirring the dust into lazy swirls. Poe grinned, rolling his shoulders, his hand resting easy on his holster. Dixon dismounted slow, stretching like this was just another day's work.

Harlan stayed on his horse, watching.

Waiting.

McKinnrick reined in, studying the rancher with that same calm, measured stare. "Morning, Thomas."

Morrissey didn't answer.

McKinnrick smiled. Not cruel, not mocking. Just patient. "I hear you've been struggling."

Morrissey's jaw worked tight. His fingers twitched once, then clenched into fists. "Ain't got nothing left to give you."

A beat.

The heat pressed in heavy, thick with something that hadn't been spoken yet.

McKinnrick let out a breath, slow and even. "That so?"

His eyes flicked to Dixon.

A single glance. That was all it took. Dixon dropped from his horse. Fast. Brutal. Efficient. His hand shot out, grabbing a fistful of Morrissey's shirt, yanking him off the porch. The rancher stumbled, his boots dragging through the dust, but he didn't fight.

Not yet.

Not until the first punch landed. It came hard and quick, a solid crack of knuckles against ribs. Morrissey grunted, coughing, doubling over slightly. But he didn't fall. Dixon hit him again—a sharp, brutal hook to the jaw that sent Morrissey staggering back, his shoulder colliding with the post.

Poe chuckled, stepping forward and tipping his hat back. "Damn. Fella's got some weight in him."

Dixon grabbed him again, driving a knee into his ribs.

That did it.

Morrissey hit the ground hard, his breath leaving him in a sharp, painful wheeze. His hands dug into the dirt, pushing up, but Poe was already on him, crouching close, one hand pressing down on the back of his neck, forcing him back into the dust.

"Maybe next time," Poe murmured, his grin sharp, "you'll remember your obligations."

Morrissey spat blood, his chest rising and falling heavy, his breath sharp and shallow. He didn't beg. Didn't say a damn word. He just glared up through the sweat and dirt, his eyes burning sharp with something that wasn't quite defiance—but wasn't broken yet either.

Harlan felt his stomach twist, not from the violence. Violence was easy. Violence made sense. It was the way McKinnrick hadn't moved. Hadn't done a damn thing but watch, patient, unmoved, like he was observing a man sharpening a knife rather than a beating.

McKinnrick swung back into his saddle. Didn't glance at Morrissey. Didn't acknowledge the man bleeding in the dust. He just adjusted his coat, settled into his seat, and said, "Come next month, I expect you to find a way."

That was it.

That was all.

Dixon stepped back, rolling his shoulders, flexing his knuckles like he was checking for any damage. Poe let out a low chuckle, clapping him on the back before turning back toward his horse.

Harlan still hadn't moved. Still hadn't spoken. Because if he said something now—if he stopped this—he knew exactly what it meant. Exactly where it would put him. So he just sat there, boots steady in the stirrups, reins loose in his grip. And let it happen. They left Morrissey lying in the dust, broken but breathing. And Harlan knew something then it was only a matter of time before he'd be asked to deliver a beating, pull a trigger, kill an innocent man.

The following day, the heat settled into the land like a slow fever, thick and unmoving. The sun hung high, a hard, white glare against a washed-out sky, sucking the moisture from the earth, leaving the ground cracked and brittle. The only shade came from the occasional scrub oak, stunted and twisted, its roots clinging deep to whatever was left beneath the surface.

The gang moved slow, their horses picking a careful path through the dry wash, the sound of hooves muffled against the packed earth. No one spoke much. The heat had a way of pressing the words out of a man, leaving him with nothing but the sound of his own breath and the creak of leather.

Dixon pulled up first, his body shifting in the saddle. "Dust," he said, his voice low but certain.

That one word changed everything. McKinnrick reined in beside him, squinting toward the horizon. Harlan followed their gaze, spotting it a moment later—a thin plume of dust curling into the air, distant but moving. The shimmer of heat made it hard to tell much more, but Harlan could make out the vague, dark shapes of riders, moving steady, cutting toward a low arroyo.

McKinnrick didn't react right away. He just watched, eyes narrow beneath the brim of his hat, his horse shifting beneath him. His face gave nothing away, but Harlan had been around him long enough to recognize the way his shoulders settled, the way his grip on the reins went just a little looser, like a man sliding into something familiar. A decision had already been made.

McKinnrick gave short nod. "Rustlers." He didn't ask. Didn't guess. Just stated it, like a fact already known.

Poe let out a low chuckle, his fingers brushing the stock of his rifle, the grin on his face just a little too sharp. "Reckon they got anything worth taking?"

McKinnrick let out a breath, slow and easy, like a man settling into a long ride. "Only one way to find out."

They moved wide, peeling off into a slow, deliberate arc, using the rise and fall of the land to their advantage. Harlan rode near the back, feeling the weight of it in his gut—the way McKinnrick's men weren't rushing, weren't concerned. They'd done this before. Enough time to know exactly how to do it again.

The terrain shifted as they rode, the land dropping into rocky gullies and low ridges, natural creases in the desert that gave just enough cover to stay out of sight. The arroyo ahead was cut deep into the land, its walls sloping down in jagged steps, the earth carved away from years of flash floods that had long since dried up.

It was the perfect place to set up camp. And the perfect place to get trapped. The rustlers were down in the wash, their horses tied off near a patch of scrub, saddles stripped, a small fire smoldering between them. There were six, maybe seven men, moving around easy, laughing, their rifles leaning against boulders within reach, but not held close. They weren't watching their backs.

Harlan's fingers curled tight around the reins. Something cold slid beneath his ribs, something instinctual. They didn't have to do this. They could ride up straight, call them out, give them a chance to talk before the bullets started flying. But that wasn't how this would go. Harlan could feel it, coiling tight in his chest. There were no stolen steers, just the men. No evidence at all that these were men on the wrong side of the law.

McKinnrick lifted his hand.

Held it still.

The men shifted, readying their guns, glancing toward him like a pack of wolves waiting for the signal to strike.

Then, without a word—

He dropped it.

For half a second, there was nothing—just the slow ripple of heat, the creak of saddle leather, the rustlers laughing low in the arroyo, still unaware that death had already found them.

And the world exploded.

The first shot cracked through the still air, sharp and clean, the sound rolling through the canyon like thunder. One of the rustlers jerked back, arms flailing, the force of the bullet sending him tumbling sideways into the dirt. A bloom of red spread across his chest, soaking his shirt, his mouth open like he wanted to say something but never got the chance.

The second shot followed fast, then another, and another. Gunfire ripped through the arroyo, the air suddenly thick with the raw scent of burnt powder and blood. The rustlers scrambled for cover, but the arroyo worked against them.

The land that had sheltered them before was now their cage. The steep walls gave them nowhere to run, and their horses reared and screamed, kicking up clouds of dust as they fought against their tethers.

One of the rustlers—a thin man in a sweat-stained hat—reached for his rifle, his fingers fumbling with the lever. The gun was up a second later and pointed towards Harlan.

Harlan's Colt was already up.

He had no choice, and he fired.

The revolver kicked hard in his grip, the blast echoing through the narrow wash. The man staggered back, his hand slapping to his gut, blood seeping through his fingers. He made a wet, choked noise, sinking to his knees before pitching forward into the dirt.

More shots rang out, each one cutting another man down. Poe let out a sharp, wild laugh, his rifle pressed tight against his shoulder.

Crack.

A rustler jerked sideways, his boots sliding in the loose dirt, his body twisting as he fell. His legs twitched once—twice—then stilled. Another man tried to make a run for his horse, his boots kicking up dust as he bolted toward the animals. McKinnrick saw him first. His gun came up smooth, unhurried.

One shot.

The man crashed forward, face-down, the earth swallowing his scream. Harlan caught a flicker of movement from the corner of his eye—a rustler who had managed to find some cover behind a low boulder, trying to work the lever on his rifle. Harlan turned, firing twice. The first shot hit the rock, chipping stone into the air. The second caught the rustler in the shoulder, spinning him around and knocking him to the ground. He was still moving, groaning, trying to reach his gun. Dixon rode closer, his boots hitting the dirt as he dismounted. The rustler looked up, one hand pressing against his wound, the other reaching for his gun.

Dixon didn't give him the chance.

He raised his revolver.

Fired once.

The man's body jerked, then went still. Dixon didn't even look twice. Just holstered his weapon, stepping over the corpse like it was nothing.

The fight didn't last long. It was never going to. It was too fast, too brutal, too one-sided. The rustlers had been caught off-guard, and McKinnrick's men had done this before. When the last rustler dropped, silence settled over the arroyo, thick and heavy, like the land itself had been holding its breath. Harlan lowered his gun, smoke curling from the barrel, his pulse still hammering in his ears.

The air was sharp with the smell of blood and dust, the ground littered with spent casings and bodies.

It was over.

Or damn near.

A rustler lay on his side, breathing hard, his leg slick with blood. His fingers trembled as he tried to push himself up, but he couldn't make it. His breath hitched, his mouth opening like he wanted to say something. Dixon walked over, his shadow falling over the dying man.

He didn't speak.

Didn't hesitate.

He just raised his gun and pulled the trigger. The rustler jerked once, then stilled, his blood leaking into the dirt. Dixon holstered his gun, adjusting his hat like he'd just finished another day's work. This wasn't a fight. This was an execution. And Harlan was part of it.

The silence that followed the gunfire was thick and heavy, settling over the arroyo like the weight of the sun pressing down on the dry land. The dust still hung in the air, curling in lazy spirals where bullets had kicked up the dirt. The scent of burnt powder and blood lingered, sharp and metallic, mixing with the sweat already clinging to Harlan's skin.

No one spoke at first.

There wasn't much left to say.

The rustlers were dead, their bodies sprawled out in the dust, some still gripping their weapons in stiff fingers, others staring up at the pale blue sky with glassy, unseeing eyes. The ones who had died clean were the lucky ones.

The others—the ones who had bled out slow, who had coughed their last breaths into the dirt, fingers twitching, eyes wide with the final realization of it all—they were still. Now part of the land. And then, without hesitation, McKinnrick's men got to work. Holsters were unbuckled. Pockets turned out.

Dixon knelt beside one of the rustlers, rolling the man onto his back with a careless shove. His fingers went straight for the dead man's coat, rifling through pockets, pulling out a few loose coins and a folded letter stained with blood. Dixon glanced at it once, then tossed it aside into the dirt.

"Damn shame," he muttered, but there was no pity in his voice.

Poe was less subtle. He moved through the bodies like a man picking apples off a tree, taking whatever looked worth taking. A handful of bills here, a decent knife there, even a half-full flask of whiskey from one of the rustlers' belts. He took a long swig, then wiped his mouth with the back of his hand, grinning through his blood-streaked beard.

Jonas Cutter crouched beside a stocky man in a torn vest, his fingers working at something tucked in the dead man's vest pocket. A moment later, he pulled out a silver pocket watch, flipping it open with a flick of his thumb. The inside was engraved, something small and neat, but Cutter didn't bother to read it.

He just laughed, low and amused. "Ain't doin' him no good now." Then he pocketed it.

One of the rustlers—a younger man, maybe barely past twenty—had fallen on his side, his body half-twisted in the dirt. His left hand was curled into a fist, tight even in death. Dixon crouched and pried the fingers apart, revealing a small gold band.

A wedding ring.

Dixon let out a slow whistle, rolling the band between his fingers, letting it catch the sunlight. "Now, what the hell you doin' wearing something like this, boy?" He shook his head, then pocketed it without another thought.

The dead man's hand flopped back into the dirt, loose and lifeless.

Harlan's jaw tightened. He hadn't moved from his saddle. Hadn't said a word. But his fingers curled tighter around the reins. McKinnrick sat his horse a little ways off, his reins held loose in his grip, his coat dusted with the grit of the fight. Watching. Not stopping them. Not joining in, either. Just watching. Like this was part of the natural order of things. Like this was how it was supposed to go. Harlan flicked his gaze toward him, trying to read something in his face. Approval? Disapproval? Nothing at all? But McKinnrick's expression was unreadable. Maybe that was worse.

Harlan sat his buckskin still, feeling the heat of the sun settling into his shoulders, his skin damp beneath his coat. He watched as boots were stripped from dead feet, as pockets were emptied without hesitation, as the last of a man's possessions were taken before the land swallowed his body whole.

He'd seen worse.

But something about this—the ease of it, the familiarity of it—sat wrong in his chest. McKinnrick's men weren't looting because they needed to. They were looting because it was a habit. Because they had done this enough times that it wasn't a question. It was expected. Harlan let out a slow breath, his fingers relaxing on the grip of his Colt. He could still feel the heat of the gunfight in his bones, could still hear the echo of the last shots, the wet sound of a man choking on his own blood.

These men weren't being punished for stealing cattle or robbing stagecoaches. They were dead, and now their bodies were just pockets to turn out. They'd been reduced to nothing more than a few coins, a pair of boots, a silver watch clutched in the fingers of a dead man.

Poe straightened up, wiping the sweat from his brow with the back of his hand. His eyes flicked over to Harlan, a slow grin curling on his lips. "What's the matter, Harlan? You look like you've seen a ghost."

Harlan didn't answer. Just stared at Poe, feeling the weight of the Colt at his side. He let out a slow breath, fighting the urge to draw, to level the barrel at Poe's face, to end that grin with a bullet and call it justice. But he didn't. He didn't move. Because if he started down that road, there wouldn't be any turning back.

McKinnrick's voice cut through the silence, low and calm. "Mount up."

The men moved quick, stowing their stolen goods, tightening their saddles. The leader's eyes were sharp and cold, like a knife's edge. He held Harlan's gaze for a second longer than he should have—just long enough to let Harlan know that he saw the doubt there, that he saw the unease clawing at him. Long enough to let Harlan know that he understood. That he saw what Harlan was thinking. That he had seen Harlan remain in his saddle and not help himself to the booty on offer.

Dixon adjusted his hat, his lip curling into a sneer as he nudged his horse forward. "Let's ride. Ain't nothin' left worth takin'."

The others followed, riding easy, leaving the bodies behind without a second thought. Poe flicked a spent cartridge into the dust, the metal glinting briefly in the sun before it disappeared into the earth.

Harlan looked down at the dead man nearest to him as he rode out—a rustler with a ragged hole in his chest, his shirt dark with blood, his eyes fixed on the sky above. There was a coin beside his outstretched hand, half-buried in the dirt. He thought about leaning down and picking it up. The thought came unwanted into his mind. Then he thought about how many men had died for less. So he left it there. He nudged his horse forward, leaving the rustlers behind, leaving the blood-soaked ground to swallow the dead.

But that tightness in his gut stayed. And he knew, deep down, that he'd made a mistake. That staying silent was the wrong choice. That one day, he was gonna have to pay for it.

They rode out of the arroyo, the heat settling behind them like the whisper of something gone rotten. Cutter's horse kicked up a spray of loose dirt, and Harlan heard the faint clink of silver—the sound of Cutter flipping the stolen pocket watch open and closed. The noise was soft, almost musical, and it sent a cold shiver down Harlan's spine.

He glanced back once—just once—watching as the bodies faded into the land, swallowed by the heat, by the dust. Then he faced forward, the reins tight in his hands, his eyes fixed on the horizon.

And he kept riding. Because if he stopped now—if he let himself think too long about what they'd done, about what they'd left behind—he might not be able to keep going. And right now, the only thing he had left was momentum. So he didn't look back again. He just kept moving forward, the shadow of death riding close behind him, like a whisper he couldn't shake. And the desert stretched on, endless and unforgiving, swallowing the echoes of gunfire and the blood-soaked memories they left behind.

CHAPTER 9: THE LAW AIN'T COMING

The night air was thick with heat, the smell of dust and dry earth hanging heavy in the dark. The moon rode high, casting a pale glow over the land, but it did nothing to soften the hard edges of the scene unfolding below. Harlan knew where they were going, a man called Eldon Briggs owed McKinnrick, and tonight they were 'doing the rounds' again.

The Briggs homestead sat low against the land, its walls weathered, the roof sagging in places. A patch of brittle grass stretched around it, fenced in with barbed wire that had seen better years. Off to the side stood the barn, an old, tired thing with wood as dry as kindling, its roof caved in slightly along one edge. The kind of barn that had seen too many summers without enough rain. Harlan rode near the back, his horse moving slow, the gang's approach measured, deliberate. They didn't rush. Didn't have to.

The people inside already knew they were coming.

Eldon Briggs stood on the porch, a lantern gripped tight in one hand, his fingers curled around the handle like it was the last solid thing he had to hold onto. He was lean, sunbaked, the kind of man whose body had been shaped by hard labor. His clothes were stiff with dust, and the lines on his face looked etched deep like they'd been carved there over years of hard luck. His wife stood behind him, barefoot in the doorway, clutching a small boy to her chest. The child's wide, frightened eyes peered out from the folds of her dress, unblinking.

Briggs knew why they were here.

Knew what was coming.

McKinnrick swung down from his saddle with the ease of a man who wasn't worried about how this was going to play out. His coat settled around him as he stepped forward, his spurs clicking lightly against the wooden steps.

He didn't reach for his gun. Didn't raise his voice. Just looked Briggs in the eye, his expression unreadable. "Eldon," McKinnrick said, slow, calm. "You missed your payment."

Briggs swallowed hard. His knuckles went white on the lantern handle. "I—" His voice hitched, then steadied. "I just need a little more time, Mister McKinnrick. Just another month."

McKinnrick let out a slow breath, nodding slightly like he was considering the request. Then he turned —not to Briggs, but to Poe and Dixon. A small gesture. A tilt of the head. That was all.

Poe grinned. Dixon spit into the dirt. Then both men swung out of their saddles, boots hitting the ground with the finality of a coffin lid slamming shut.

Briggs stiffened. "Wait—"

Poe and Dixon didn't wait.

They strode toward the barn.

Briggs moved fast, stepping off the porch, the lantern swinging wildly in his grip. "Please,

McKinnrick—don't do this! I swear, I'll have it next time! Just a few more weeks!"

McKinnrick didn't answer. Didn't even look at him. Just stood there, waiting. Poe reached into his saddlebag, pulling out a glass bottle with a rag stuffed in the top. Harlan didn't have to ask what was inside. Dixon already had his flint out. The barn doors creaked in the breeze, the dry wood groaning like it already knew what was coming.

The first torch hit the side of the barn, the flames catching fast, licking their way up the warped planks. The fire grew quick, climbing the old, dried-out beams, eating through the wood like a starving thing. The lantern in Briggs' hand crashed to the ground, the glass shattering, oil spreading dark across the dirt. He stumbled forward, reaching toward the barn, but Dixon was on him in an instant, grabbing a fistful of his shirt and yanking him backward.

"No, no, NO—"

Dixon threw him hard into the dirt, sending the breath from his lungs in a sharp, choked gasp. His wife screamed from the doorway, her voice raw, her arms tightening around the child, who was now sobbing against her chest.

Briggs tried to push up, his hands clawing at the ground. Dixon stomped a boot down on his chest, pinning him there. "Don't be stupid, Eldon."

The flames swallowed the barn now, roaring high into the night, black smoke curling into the sky. Inside, the cattle trapped in the stalls began to scream, hooves kicking against the wooden walls, panic bleeding into the fire-lit darkness. Harlan clenched his jaw, his grip tightening on the reins.

The sound was worse than gunfire. Worse than the dying gasps of men he'd put down. Because those animals knew. They understood, in some deep, primal way, that this was the end.

The barn roof collapsed, sending a spray of glowing embers into the sky, the heat pulsing outward in thick, suffocating waves.

Briggs stopped struggling. Stopped begging.

Just lay there, pinned in the dirt, watching his livelihood burn.

McKinnrick watched the fire for a moment longer, then turned, stepping back toward his horse. Briggs was still staring, his face slack, his eyes reflecting the orange glow of everything he'd worked for turning to ash. McKinnrick settled into his saddle, adjusting his coat. Then he looked down at Briggs, his voice as calm as if he were discussing the weather.

"Next time, don't make me come back."

Briggs didn't respond. Didn't even look at him. Just kept staring at the flames. McKinnrick gave a short nod, then turned his horse. The others followed Poe and Dixon laughing as they swung up into their saddles, Cutter flipping that damn pocket watch open and closed, the faint clink of metal barely audible over the crackle of the fire. Harlan nudged his horse forward, his stomach twisting, the smoke thick in his throat.

He glanced once—just once—at the farmhouse, at the woman still standing in the doorway, her face pale, her hands clamped tight around her child. At Briggs, motionless in the dirt, his breathing shallow, his face unreadable. The barn burned bright behind them, throwing long, flickering shadows across the land as they rode away.

And Harlan knew—deep in his bones—

This wasn't a lesson.

It was a warning.

And sooner or later, someone was gonna come back for more than just a barn.

The fire cracked low, curling thin wisps of smoke into the night air, but Harlan could still taste the last fire on the back of his tongue. The barn. The dry wood catching like paper. The cattle screaming inside. It sat thick in his throat, a phantom of ash and heat that wouldn't fade, no matter how many times he swallowed.

He sat on a flat rock just outside the firelight, rolling a cigarette slow between his fingers, letting the tobacco settle even though he knew it wouldn't do much for him. The act was habit—something to keep his hands busy, something to keep his mind from turning circles around the thing he wasn't ready to say out loud. He struck a match against his boot, held the flame to the tip, took a long pull. The smoke curled out between his teeth, but it didn't calm him the way it used to.

Nothing did these days.

The gang was scattered around the fire, sprawled across the dirt like they had no weight to carry, no ghosts pressing on their shoulders. Dixon and Poe were passing a bottle back and forth, laughing like they'd just come from a good card game, not from burning a man's livelihood to the ground. Poe swung his boots up on a log, tipping his head back to take a deep swallow of whiskey before wiping his mouth with the back of his hand. "Did you see his face?" He let out a sharp, barking laugh. "Goddamn, I thought the poor bastard was gonna piss himself."

Dixon chuckled, flicking a loose ember from the hem of his coat. "Next time, he'll pay on time."

Next time. Like it was already set in stone. Like they already knew there would be a next time.

Cutter sat a little apart from them, leaning against his saddle, absently flipping his silver pocket watch open and closed, the soft clink of the metal almost rhythmic, steady as a heartbeat.

Open. Shut.

Open. Shut.

The firelight caught the engraved surface, throwing flickers of silver into the dark. Harlan had never seen Cutter check the time on that damn thing. It didn't seem like that was what it was for. The others told stories, old tales from when they rode with Quantrill rustled horses, or gunned down men they barely remembered the names of. They spoke about it all like it was just work.

A life without consequence.

Without weight.

Harlan exhaled slowly, tapping ash from his cigarette, his gaze slipping over the men around the fire. This ain't where I belong. He felt it now, more than ever. He'd told himself before that it was just a job. That he was here because he didn't have a choice. But that was a lie, wasn't it? He could have left. He could have turned his horse toward the open country, and lost himself somewhere beyond McKinnrick's reach. But he hadn't. He'd stayed.

And now, every mile he rode with them, every fire he sat around, made it harder to walk away.

But leaving wasn't simple.

Not anymore.

Not when Garrison was waiting with a noose.

Not when he had nowhere else to go.

Harlan took another slow drag, feeling the burn settle deep in his lungs, but it didn't help. Didn't steady the thing turning over and over in his chest. He'd seen it before—men who stayed too long in the wrong place, let themselves sink in too deep until there was no digging their way out. And for the first time since he'd fallen in with McKinnrick's crew, he realized he might be one of them.

He glanced over at McKinnrick, who was sitting just outside the fire's glow, his face unreadable, his hat pulled low over his brow.

He wasn't laughing.

Wasn't drinking.

Just watching.

Watching Harlan. Like he already knew what he was thinking. Like he'd seen this story play out before. The thought gnawed at Harlan, but he didn't speak it aloud. Not yet.

The fire had burned low, its glow casting long, flickering shadows across the ground, throwing just enough light to make the night feel thinner but not enough to chase away the weight in Harlan's chest. The voices around camp had quieted. Dixon and Poe had drunk themselves into a lazy half-stupor, their conversation turning to slurred mutterings. Cutter still flipped that damn pocket watch open and shut, but even that had slowed, his eyelids drooping, his breathing steady.

The men who had spent the night laughing and drinking, sharing stories of blood and stolen things, had begun to drift toward sleep, sprawling out beside saddles and blankets, their boots still on, their guns within reach.

All except McKinnrick. He was still watching. Still awake. And he was staring straight at Harlan. "Somethin' on your mind, Harlan?" McKinnrick's voice was quiet, but it carried through the night, low and deliberate, cutting through the crackle of the fire.

Harlan didn't answer at first. He just rolled the cigarette between his fingers, felt the rough paper against his skin, let the ember at the tip smolder down to nothing. Then, finally—

"Ain't what I signed up for."

McKinnrick smirked. A slow, knowing thing. "Ain't that the way?"

Harlan shook his head, exhaled smoke, watching it curl up into the dark, lost among the stars. "I don't burn down barns for a livin'."

McKinnrick leaned forward, elbows on his knees, his expression unreadable. "You think the law's gonna take you in, give you a warm bed?" His voice was calm. No judgment in it. Just fact. "You're already too deep in, son."

The words sat between them, heavy, unmoving.

Harlan didn't respond because what the hell was there to say?

McKinnrick wasn't wrong. He wasn't trying to scare him. He didn't have to. Because Harlan had known it since the moment he'd sat in that Garrison jail cell, the gallows waiting for him outside. The law wasn't coming to save him. And if he left this gang now, he wasn't riding into some clean slate, fresh start. He was just another man on the run. Another stray dog looking for a place to lay low, knowing damn well there weren't no such thing.

McKinnrick watched him a moment longer, then leaned back, his face shadowed in the dim firelight. "You walk away now, you're just another dead man waitin' to happen. And you don't got many places left to run to."

The fire popped.

The embers flared for a brief moment, sending a slow drift of orange sparks up into the black sky.

Harlan held McKinnrick's gaze.

McKinnrick didn't blink.

Didn't press the issue.

He didn't need to.

The decision had already been made.

Maybe not out loud. Maybe not yet.

But they both knew how this was gonna play out.

Finally, Harlan leaned back, adjusting his hat lower over his eyes. He didn't say a word. McKinnrick gave a small nod like he knew Harlan would come to the right conclusion.

Then, softly— "Get some sleep. We ride at first light."

Harlan stretched out, his back against the hard-packed dirt, his hat tilted low, the weight of it pressing just enough to shut the world out. The smell of smoke still clung to his clothes, the barn fire still burned behind his eyes when he closed them. He told himself he was sticking around because he had to. Because there wasn't any other choice. Because McKinnrick was right. But deep down, he knew the truth. There ain't no way this ends quiet. There ain't no way this ends without blood.

And sooner or later—

He's gonna have to pick a side.

CHAPTER 10: A DANGEROUS PROPOSITION

The fire burned steady, casting a dim orange glow against the wide stretch of desert. It wasn't much, just enough to keep the night's chill at bay, but no one seemed to mind. McKinnrick had been gone two days. Said he had business. Didn't say what, didn't say where. Just rode out and left them to their own devices. The men were in no hurry to question it.

Waiting wasn't so bad when there was whiskey to drink, cards to play, and no one breathing down their necks about where they had to be next.

Poe and Dixon sat in the dirt, hunched over a deck of cards, the pot between them growing as the night wore on. Cutter lounged against a saddle, flipping open his pocket watch, snapping it shut again, his eyes distant, like he was counting time in a way only he understood. A few of the others stretched out in the heat, boots kicked up, lazy from the long days behind them and the ease of a rare moment where no one had to move unless they felt like it.

Someone muttered something about a woman in Tucson. Someone else grunted a half-laugh and told him to shut the hell up. The whiskey passed slowly, each man taking a pull before sending it along. Harlan sat just outside the firelight, rolling a cigarette, slow and steady, letting the act settle his nerves. The night was clear, the stars sharp overhead, and the desert stretched out all around them, vast and empty. The kind of quiet that could make a man forget how much blood he'd spilled.

The fire had burned low, the embers glowing red in the deep dark of the desert. The night was still, the only sound the occasional murmur of voices, the scrape of a match lighting a cigarette, the distant yawn of the wind curling through the brush.

Harlan sat with his back to a rock, half-listening to Poe and Dixon argue over the last poker hand, their voices easy, unhurried. Cutter sat cross-legged, absently flipping his pocket watch open and shut, the steady *click* the only measure of time passing.

Then—hoofbeats. Slow at first. Distant. Then closer.

The conversation died off like a candle snuffed in the wind.

Men shifted some stretching toward their guns out of habit, others just turning their heads toward the sound, watching.

McKinnrick rode into camp like he was returning to a place he owned.

His stallion moved smooth, steady, its coat streaked with dust from the road. McKinnrick himself looked the same as always—hat pulled low, coat settled sharply across his shoulders, his gun riding easy on his hip.

He didn't say a word as he swung down, dusted off his coat, and tied his reins loose to a low mesquite branch.

For a long second, no one spoke.

Then McKinnrick stepped forward, the firelight catching in his eyes, and a slow grin spread across his face.

"Well, boys," he drawled, "miss me?"

Dixon chuckled low, pulling at the whiskey bottle and tossing it across the fire toward McKinnrick, who caught it without effort.

"Hell, I was startin' to think you run off," Poe muttered, exhaling smoke.

McKinnrick just smirked, tipping the bottle back for a long pull before lowering it. "You think too much, Poe."

He stepped closer to the fire, stretching, rolling his shoulders like a man shaking off a long ride. He didn't immediately tell them where he'd been. Didn't immediately say what the next move was.

Because he didn't have to.

They all knew he'd have a job for them soon enough.

Instead, he let the whiskey settle in his gut, let the firelight dance in his eyes, and let them wait.

Because McKinnrick never wasted words.

And when he did speak, it always meant something.

McKinnrick cleared his throat. And the whole camp changed. The murmured conversation cut off like a blade through rope. A few heads turned. No one spoke. Because when McKinnrick talked, it meant something. He wasn't the type to waste words.

"I got us a job." His voice was low and deliberate, each word measured out with purpose like he'd already made up his mind and was just letting the rest of them in on it.

He let the words hang, scanning the men in the firelight, watching their faces, their reactions.

No one spoke yet.

They were waiting.

Waiting for him to tell them how deep they were about to go.

McKinnrick took his time, pulling a thin cigar from inside his coat, striking a match against the heel of his boot. The flame flared bright for an instant, throwing deep lines across his face before he cupped his hand around it, drawing in slow.

Then he let the match drop, the tiny ember dying in the dirt. "Army payroll shipment," he said, exhaling smoke.

A shift in the circle.

A few glances exchanged.

Not fear. Not hesitation.

Just awareness.

This wasn't some half-drunk rancher who needed reminding to pay up. This wasn't some rustler getting what was coming to him. This was the Army.

McKinnrick continued, voice steady. "Strongbox full of Union gold. Fort McCall to a supply depot out east.

That got their attention. Harlan straightened slightly, Cutter stopped flipping his damn pocket watch, and even Poe—who usually acted like he had one boot in the grave already—sat forward, and Dixon grinned like a mad coyote.

"How many guards?" Cutter asked.

McKinnrick didn't blink. "Six, maybe seven. Couple of riders, maybe a sergeant running the show. But it's just a transport. They ain't expecting trouble."

The men started murmuring, the low hum of excitement settling in now.

Gold.

Not cattle. Not whiskey.

Not a rancher's last handful of coins shoved into a shaking fist.

Gold.

McKinnrick let the talk go for a second, let them feel it, let them start tasting the weight of what they were about to take. Then he cut back in, voice firm. "We take that gold, we can ride easy for a long while. No more pocket change from scared ranchers. No more scraping by."

Poe chuckled. "Shit, we could buy our own damn town."

Cutter smirked, snapping his pocket watch closed. "That's if we don't get strung up first."

That brought a few low laughs.

But nobody disagreed.

McKinnrick sat near the flames, legs stretched out, his coat loose around his shoulders, dust still clinging to the hem. He took his time, rolling the whiskey in his palm, letting the silence stretch just long enough to make them lean in. Then, finally, he spoke. "I got us a man on the inside."

Dixon raised a brow. "Inside what?"

McKinnrick's smirk was slow, like he was enjoying the weight of his own words. He took a sip before answering. "Army's been running shipments through the territory, moving payroll for the forts up north. They keep it light, a couple of wagons, maybe a half-dozen men. Nothing we can't handle. But this one—this one's special." He glanced at them over the rim of his glass. "This one, we know about ahead of time."

Cutter frowned. "And how the hell do we know that?"

McKinnrick grinned, tapping a finger against the whiskey bottle. "Like I said. I got a man on the inside."

Harlan felt something shift in his gut. He wasn't sure if it was unease or anticipation.

McKinnrick leaned forward, his voice lowering, making them listen close. "Name's Porter. Captain. Been in the Army long enough to know it don't pay near as good as it should. He's been feeding me information for a while now—locations, shipments, troop movements. Man's got a taste for finer things, and Uncle Sam don't pay for whiskey or women." He took another sip, smirking. "But I do."

Poe chuckled low. "So what's he givin' us?"

McKinnrick set the bottle down between his boots, fingers drumming against the glass.

"A wagon, two weeks from now. Heading through Devil's Pass. Strongbox full of gold meant for Fort McCall. Escort's light—maybe seven, eight men." He let that sink in. "We hit it hard, take the gold, and by the time the Army knows what happened, we'll be long gone."

Dixon let out a low whistle. "Hell of a score."

McKinnrick just smiled. "Hell of a payout."

Harlan shifted slightly, the words settling in his mind.

A man on the inside. A captain. That was different from hunting wanted men. Different from shaking down ranchers for what they owed. This was a heist. But he didn't say that. Instead, he just nodded, watching McKinnrick carefully. "Sounds like a plan."

Because what else was he supposed to say?

Harlan watched them all, his cigarette burning slow between his fingers. They were already bought in. Already seeing the gold in their pockets, already planning how they'd spend it. But Harlan wasn't so sure. Something about this sat wrong in his gut. Not the danger. Not the killing. That part he could live with. But robbing the Army? That wasn't the same as some outlaw gang. That wasn't the same as some poor bastard trying to hold onto his last few dollars.

The Army didn't just send a few men after you. They didn't just file a report and let it go. They hunted you. Tracked you. Ran you into the ground until there wasn't a damn thing left to bury. And McKinnrick knew it. But he wasn't saying it. Not yet.

Harlan flicked his cigarette into the dirt, watching the glow fade. He didn't say a word. Because he already knew McKinnrick wouldn't be swayed.

The men were still murmuring to themselves, half-drunk on whiskey and the thought of gold in their pockets, a fresh start, a score big enough to mean something. Dixon had already run the numbers out loud—how much each man would take, how far that could get them. Poe laughed between swigs, already talking about what town he'd spend his cut in, which saloon, which women.

Harlon thumbed the cigarette's edge, packing the tobacco in tighter, felt the tension creeping up his spine. And then, finally, he spoke. "You're talkin' about robbin' soldiers, McKinnrick." His voice was steady, low. "That ain't the same as some rustlers in a canyon."

The words hung in the air, slicing through the low hum of conversation.

A few heads turned. The firelight flickered in McKinnrick's eyes. Unmoving. Unreadable.

"You think the Army's just gonna let that go?" Harlan continued.

Silence settled around the camp. The fire cracked again, the only sound for a long stretch.

Then McKinnrick smiled. Just a little. "You afraid of soldiers, Harlan?"

Harlan took his time. He struck a match on his boot, cupped it with his hand against the wind, let the flame catch the end of the cigarette before shaking it out. He took a slow drag, exhaling the smoke toward the fire before finally answering. "I ain't afraid of 'em." His voice was even. Steady. But he let the pause stretch before he added, "But I ain't stupid either."

McKinnrick's smile faded just a fraction.

Harlan tapped ash into the dirt. "Army, don't just send a few men after you." His voice was quieter now, more like a fact than an argument. "You pull a job like this, they come huntin'." His eyes locked on McKinnrick's, but the leader didn't flinch. Didn't move. "And they don't stop."

The air tightened around the camp.

The men had stopped their talking. Some of them glanced between McKinnrick and Harlan, waiting to see which way the wind was gonna blow.

Cutter snorted, breaking the silence, flicking his pocket watch open and closed. "Hell," he muttered, shaking his head. "We already got the law on our backs in a few states. What's a few blue-bellies?"

A few of the others chuckled, shaking off the tension. But Harlan didn't smile. Because he knew this wasn't the same. Not by a long shot.

McKinnrick hadn't moved much, hadn't raised his voice, hadn't even reached for his gun. He didn't need to. He just leaned forward, elbows resting on his knees, hands hanging loose, looking at Harlan like a man who'd already made his decision and was there waiting for everyone else to catch up. "There's risk in everything, Harlan." His voice was calm, even the kind of tone men used when they weren't asking—they were telling. "But I ain't been wrong yet."

Harlan let out a slow breath through his nose, keeping his expression flat, unreadable. He'd heard that line before. Hell, every leader who ever led men into a fight they couldn't walk away from said thc same thing. I ain't been wrong yet. Right up until the day they were. McKinnrick knew the risks. Knew exactly what he was leading them into. And he didn't care. Or worse—he did, but he wasn't going to let it change his course.

The flames licked along the logs, turning the wood black, the heat wrapping tight around them, thick as the weight of what McKinnrick was proposing.

"We do this right, we don't leave no trail behind." McKinnrick's eyes flickered in the firelight, but they never wavered. "We take the gold, split it up, and ride separate for a while."

His voice didn't hold doubt. Didn't hold hesitation. Just certainty. Like this was already done, already decided. Like they were just sitting here, drinking whiskey, waiting for time to catch up with it.

"By the time the Army knows what hit 'em," McKinnrick said, his lips curling slightly, "we'll be long gone."

Harlan watched him.

Watched him the way a man watches a poker player across the table, trying to find the tell, the slip, the thing that lets you know he ain't holding what he says he is. But McKinnrick was steady. No nervous twitch. No flicker of doubt. He believed it. And Harlan knew, right then and there, that there wasn't gonna be any talking him out of it. McKinnrick had already made up his mind, the job was happening.

"Two days." McKinnrick's voice was even measured. "That's what we got."

The men listened, waiting. There was no arguing now.

"The payroll wagon moves at first light, passing through Devil's Pass by noon." His eyes flicked to Harlan, just for a second, then back to the others. "We'll hit 'em hard and fast. No room for second chances."

The map in Harlan's head unfurled before McKinnrick even said the words. Devil's Pass. A narrow stretch of twisting canyon walls, where the rock came in tight, and the sun barely reached the ground at high noon. A place made for ambushes, for killing. One way in. One way out.

McKinnrick leaned forward, elbows on his knees. "We take position at the ridge. Wagon comes in, we light 'em up. Soldiers go down, we move in fast, take the gold, and disappear before the dust settles."

Simple.

Direct.

Like stepping on a rattlesnake's neck and thinking it'd just lie there and take it.

Dixon cracked his knuckles, grinning like he could already feel the weight of gold in his pockets. "Hell, sounds like a payday."

Poe laughed, tilting back the whiskey bottle and swallowing deeply before wiping his mouth on his sleeve. "Hope them boys said their prayers."

A few of the others chuckled, nodding, the tension cracking just enough to let in that ugly kind of excitement. The kind that always showed up right before blood got spilled.

Later, long after the men had settled in, their breathing even, the fire burning down to nothing but embers, Harlan lay awake, staring at thc sky. The stars stretched sharp and endless above him, bright against the black. The desert was quiet, save for the crackle of dying flames and the distant, restless sound of horses shifting in the brush. He told himself he had no choice but to see this through. That he was in too deep now to turn back. But deep down, he knew better.

Harlan hadn't forgotten Cutter's words.

We already got the law on our backs in a few states. What's a few blue-bellies?

The others had laughed, let the whiskey smooth over the weight of what was being said. But for Harlan, the line had been crossed. He had suspected, had seen the cracks in McKinnrick's badge, but now there was no doubt. McKinnrick wasn't just playing both sides. He was an outlaw.

Harlan waited until the fire burned low, until most of the men had turned in, then found Cutter sitting on an upturned saddle near the edge of camp, rolling a smoke. The light from the fire caught the glint of his pocket watch as he flicked it open and shut, that same slow, steady rhythm.

Harlan stepped up, arms crossed, boots kicking at the dry earth. "That true?"

Cutter didn't look up. "What's that?"

Harlan's jaw tensed. "What you said back there. About already having the law on our backs."

Cutter took his time, struck a match, let the flame catch on the end of his cigarette before shaking it out. He exhaled slow.

"Depends," he said, squinting up at Harlan. "You askin' 'cause you're just now figurin' it out? Or askin' 'cause you already knew?"

Harlan's hands curled into fists at his sides. "Just tell me."

Cutter smirked, shaking his head like he found the whole thing amusing. "McKinnrick ran the same game up north," he said, stretching his legs out. "Called himself Wells then. Started out like he always does—huntin' bad men, cleanin' up the lawless, makin' folks feel safe." Cutter let out a slow breath. "And then he started pushing the line."

Harlan frowned. "How far?"

Cutter met his gaze, the smirk gone now. "Far enough that there's a price on his head. Sheriff's office up in Kansas still got a bounty out. Dead or alive. Some of the boys got prices as well, Poe's worth more than Dixon, and he never lets him forget it."

Harlan's gut went cold. "And the gang?"

"Moved south," Cutter said. "New name, new territory. So far, no one's made the connection." He tapped the side of his watch. "But it won't be long."

Harlan stared into the dark, jaw tight. "The boys know?"

Cutter gave a slow nod. "Most of 'em." He took another drag from his smoke, his voice quieter now. "That's why the big payout matters. One good haul, enough to split town before the past catches up." He let the words settle, then glanced up at Harlan. "Might be time you start askin' yourself where you stand."

Harlan didn't answer.

Didn't know how to.

Because there was no undoing what he knew now.

CHAPTER 11: THE SET-UP

The sun was barely over the ridge, spilling thin gold light across the jagged canyon walls, turning the rock a pale, sickly yellow. The shadows were still deep in the crevices, stretching long across the pass, swallowing the spaces where the light hadn't yet reached. It was the kind of morning that made everything feel sharper.

The gang rode in slow, hooves scuffing over loose rock, wagon wheels leaving faint trails in the dust where stagecoaches had passed before. There was no breeze, no shift in the dry desert air, just a stillness that pressed down against their backs like a heavy hand. No birds on the cliffs. No wind moving through the narrow gaps in the rock. Just silence.

McKinnrick raised a hand, signaling a stop. The gang obeyed without question. No hesitation. No talking. Just the sound of leather creaking as they reined in their horses. Harlan pulled up near the back, eyes scanning the land, feeling the quiet settle into his bones.

McKinnrick turned in his saddle, nodding toward the ridge. "We'll wait here. Be ready."

His voice was calm. Sure. Like he'd already played this whole thing out in his head, already seen how it was gonna end. He swung off his horse, motioning the others into place.

They split off fast, each man moving like he already knew his role. Poe and Dixon climbed up the ridge, boots crunching over loose gravel as they found their spots behind the natural outcrops of stone. Harlan could already picture them—lying low, rifles propped on the rocks, fingers near the triggers, waiting for McKinnrick's signal. Cutter and Kearney took the bends below, near the choke point where the canyon narrowed so tight that a wagon couldn't turn around even if it wanted to. They wouldn't fire first. Their job was to close in after the shooting started and make sure no one got out alive.

Harlan stayed near McKinnrick, his horse tied further back with the others, kept out of sight. McKinnrick stood near a rocky overhang, one boot braced against a boulder, arms crossed as he scanned the road below.

Watching.

Waiting.

Calculating.

Harlan had seen him like this before. Weighing the world in his mind, turning the angles, measuring the risk. And yet, something felt wrong. Harlan didn't take his eyes off the road. He knew how an ambush worked. Knew the way tension should build before the attack, knew how silence could hum with anticipation—like the breath before a gunfight, the heartbeat before a man draws. But this wasn't that. This silence felt wrong. Hollow. Like they weren't the only ones watching.

McKinnrick adjusted his stance, fingers drumming lightly on his holster.

Dixon, up on the ridge, spit into the dirt and muttered, "Where the hell are they?"

The sun crawled higher, pushing the shadows back against the canyon walls, turning the rock into slabs of pale fire. Heat rolled off the ground in slow, rippling waves, the air thick with dust and the scent of dry sage settling into the back of Harlan's throat. Still, they waited. Time stretched, slow and uneasy, the kind of waiting that put a knot in a man's gut. The kind that made his fingers twitch toward his gun just to have something to hold onto.

The men started shifting in their spots, adjusting their grips, rolling stiff shoulders, and checking the chambers of their guns like they hadn't already done it three times over. Nobody spoke much. Even Poe—who was never short on something to say—just kept his fingers loose near his rifle, eyes flicking between the ridgeline and McKinnrick.

Harlan could hear the soft creak of Cutter's saddle leather as he leaned forward against the rock, the slow click-click of his pocket watch opening and closing. A nervous habit, but the man didn't even seem aware he was doing it.

Harlan let out a slow breath, eyes fixed on the road below.

Listening.

And what he didn't hear bothered him more than anything.

There should've been birds moving through the cliffs, wings catching the drafts between the stone. There should've been wind slipping through the canyon, whistling low through the gaps in the rock. Hell, even the horses tied back behind the ridge should've been shifting more, flicking their tails against the flies, snorting at the heat. But there was nothing. Just a hollow, unnatural stillness. Like the whole damn place was holding its breath.

Dixon muttered from his perch, voice low, wary. "Where the hell are they?"

Nobody answered. Because none of them knew. And because every one of them was starting to feel it now. That slow, creeping sense that something was wrong. That they weren't alone.

McKinnrick stood still as stone, his hands resting loose on his knees, watching the road like a man watching a card game he already knew the outcome of. His expression didn't shift. Didn't show if he felt it too. Didn't show anything at all. And that made Harlan even more uneasy.

The first sign of them was the dust. A faint plume on the horizon, barely visible at first, just a thin ribbon of smoke-colored haze curling up into the heat-heavy sky. It rose slow and deliberate, not the wild scatter of a wagon running fast but something controlled, something measured. Harlan stiffened, his eyes narrowing as he watched it. A moment later, he heard the low, rhythmic beat of hooves, the distant groan of wagon wheels grinding against the dry-packed earth. The sound drifted up through the canyon, carried on the dead stillness like a warning.

The men tensed in their spots.

He saw Dixon shift against the rock, his grip tightening around the long barrel of his rifle. Poe muttered something under his breath, adjusting his aim, the sun flashing a sharp glint of steel along his sights. Cutter stopped clicking his pocket watch, the silence that followed almost louder than the sound itself.

Harlan felt the weight in his chest grow heavier.

Something was wrong.

Then, the wagon came into view. It rolled out of the heat shimmer, its form twisting in the mirage before it settled solid and real, trundling along the winding path of the pass. But this wasn't what he'd expected. This wasn't some rickety payroll transport, a quick hit with a few guards too green or too lazy to fight back. This was something else.

The stage was reinforced with heavy iron bracing along the sides and thick wheels built for carrying weight. The kind of weight that mattered. The two horses pulling it weren't lathered or straining. They moved steady, controlled as if their riders weren't in any particular hurry.

And it wasn't alone.

More riders than there should've been. The original plan had accounted for six, maybe seven men guarding the wagon. A few soldiers, maybe a hired gun, were riding alongside. Enough to put up a fight but not enough to hold their ground once the first shots were fired.

But now Harlan counted fifteen men. They rode in a loose formation, spread just enough to keep space between them but close enough to move together when the time came. Not just guards. Soldiers. They weren't escorting a payroll wagon. They were waiting for something. Harlan felt it deep in his gut, a cold certainty curling tight behind his ribs.

This wasn't right. This wasn't how a job like this was supposed to go. And McKinnrick had to see it, too.

Harlan turned his head, about to speak—
Too late.

McKinnrick raised his hand. Then dropped it. The first shot cracked the stillness.

And all hell broke loose.

CHAPTER 12: THE TRAP IS SPRUNG

The first shot cracked through the canyon like a whip, the sound ricocheting off the stone walls, snapping the silence in two. For a heartbeat, everything held still. The dust hanging in the air. The heat pressing down like a weight. The horses shifting under their riders, sensing the violence that hadn't fully broken yet. Then, the world went straight to hell.

A thunder of gunfire erupted all at once, drowning out everything else. Muzzle flashes flared like heat lightning, sharp and blinding in the dry, yellow light. The soldiers didn't scramble or panic. They didn't jerk their horses around in confusion like greenhorns caught off guard.

They knew.

They'd been waiting.

The first three men off their saddles hit the ground running. One rolled straight behind a jagged rock outcrop, rifle already swinging up. Another ducked behind the wagon, kneeling low, his carbine braced against the iron plating. A third, an older man with sergeant's stripes faded into his uniform, stayed in the saddle just long enough to pull his pistol and fire straight up toward the ridge.

Then, the wagon itself came alive.

Small windows slid open, barely wider than a hand but just enough for rifle barrels to punch through. Before Harlan could shout a warning, gunfire erupted from inside the wagon, sharp and relentless, bullets tearing up the ridge above. Dixon swore as a shot clipped the rock beside him, spraying chips of stone across his face. Cutter ducked lower, rifle raised, but he hesitated—there was no clean shot inside that iron-plated beast.

McKinnrick cursed under his breath, ducking back as another round split the air just past his head. They couldn't take out the soldiers inside. And the rest of the escort was using the wagon as cover, tight against its reinforced sides, firing carefully, controlled like they'd planned for this very moment.

The ambush had flipped. Now, they were the ones caught out in the open.

A shot ricocheted off stone, sending sharp flecks of rock flying through the air, stinging against Harlan's cheek as he hit the ground. He landed hard, the dry grit scraping his palms, the heat of the dirt radiating through his clothes. The crack of rifles echoed through the pass, bullets slamming into the rock walls, kicking up dust, shattering loose bits of stone. Somewhere to his left, Dixon swore loud and ragged, scrambling for cover, his rifle jamming as he tried to return fire.

Poe was already laughing, even as a bullet shaved a line through his hat. "Son of a bitch! They were waitin' for us!"

No one had time to respond. Another shot split the air, and this one found its mark—Up on the ridge, Kearney jerked sideways with a sharp grunt, dropping his rifle, a dark stain blooming across his shirt. He hit the dirt, rolling once before he stopped moving.

McKinnrick's voice cut through the chaos, sharp and steady. "Get some damn cover!"

Harlan was already moving, his Colt clearing leather as he half-crawled, half-threw himself behind a boulder. A round slammed into the rock just beside his head, sending a spray of pulverized dust into his face. This wasn't just bad luck. This was a setup. And now they were in the thick of it.

Gunfire roared through the canyon, a deafening storm of lead and thunder. The air turned thick—gunpowder, dust, and smoke curling in the heat like fog, choking out the sun. The acrid sting of it filled Harlan's nose, burned the back of his throat, stung his eyes.

He blinked hard, his back pressed against the rough, sun-scorched rock, the heat of it baking through his shirt. The ground vibrated with every shot, every impact. The whole canyon had turned into a killing box.

And they were on the wrong end of it. Up on the ridge, Dixon fired first.

His rifle cracked, a sharp retort that cut through the chaos, and Harlan saw one of the soldiers stumble—a dark spray arcing through the air as the man folded against the side of the wagon. But the moment Dixon shifted for another shot, a soldier's carbine answered. The bullet slammed through his shoulder, a clean punch of lead and bone. Dixon jerked back violently, his rifle slipping from his grasp as he spun sideways, crashing onto the rocky ledge. He let out a hoarse, breathless noise, one hand clutching at the wound, dark red spilling through his fingers.

Poe took aim next, but his goddamn luck finally ran out. A bullet ripped through the air just inches from his head, slicing through his hat and sending it spinning into the dust.

"Shit!" Poe ducked low, slamming his back against the rock face, his breath coming quick and ragged. He patted at his head, as if checking if the bullet had found anything more important.

Harlan could hear him laughing under his breath, wild and jittery.

"That was close."

It wasn't funny.

But it was Poe, so of course he laughed.

Cutter wasn't as lucky. He tried to reposition, crouching low, moving for better cover. His pistol was already in hand, eyes locked on one of the soldiers behind the wagon. But he didn't make it. A shot ripped through his gut. A dull, wet thud. His body folded inward, his breath coming out in a sharp, shocked gasp. The revolver slipped from his fingers as he doubled over, one hand gripping at his stomach, trying to hold in what was spilling out.

He hit the dirt hard, curling onto his side.

And he didn't get back up.

Harlan gritted his teeth. He had to move. He turned, Colt raised, sighting one of the soldiers who had pressed too far ahead.

Breathe.

Squeeze.

The revolver kicked back hard, the familiar jolt rattling up his arm. The bullet hit just above the man's collarbone. A split-second of staggering, hands reaching instinctively for the wound. Blood bubbled at the man's lips as he fell backward, his body folding over itself in the dust. Harlan barely had time to see him hit the ground before another soldier took his place.

Too many.

Too organized.

Harlan reloaded fast, his fingers slick with sweat, his heartbeat hammering against his ribs. McKinnrick had led them straight into hell. And they weren't getting out clean. Harlan scanned the battlefield, sweat running cold down his spine despite the heat pressing down from the canyon walls. The air was thick with the sharp stink of gunpowder, blood, and dust, and the roar of gunfire was deafening—bullets snapping off stone, ricocheting wild, cutting the air close enough to feel.

He forced himself to look past the chaos. Past the deafening blasts and the screaming horses. And that's when he saw it. Movement in the rocks behind them. Not just one man. Not just a couple of stragglers working their way in.

More.

A whole damn flanking line. They weren't just caught in a bad fight. They were surrounded. This wasn't an ambush. It was a goddamn slaughter. A sharp crack split the air, and Harlan's head snapped toward the ridge. He saw a figure moving low along the rocks, rifle in hand, boots kicking loose gravel as he edged forward. Not just another soldier caught in the fight.

An Army scout.

He moved slow and deliberate, keeping his body tight to the rocks, the way a man moves when he ain't just shooting wild—he's picking his mark. And Harlan saw who that mark was.

McKinnrick.

The scout raised his carbine, sighting in steady, finger curling around the trigger. McKinnrick didn't see him. Didn't hear the grind of boots on loose dirt above him. Didn't feel the set of eyes that had already written his death down in the dust.

Harlan acted on instinct. His Colt was already up before he had time to think. A sharp pull of the trigger, a deafening boom— The scout jerked violently backward, his rifle spinning from his hands as he staggered against the rock. For a second, he stayed upright, his body fighting what his mind hadn't caught up to yet. Then his legs gave out. He crumpled hard, hitting the ridge with a dull thud, sliding a few feet before coming to a dead stop.

One down.

But it don't mean much.

Because Harlan had no time to celebrate, no time to breathe.

The next shot was already coming, a bullet snapping just past his shoulder, chipping the stone beside him. He dropped low, grit in his teeth, heart hammering. McKinnrick's men were dropping, one by one. Dixon was still bleeding on the rocks. Cutter was face-down in the dirt, unmoving. Poe was laughing between shots, but his aim was wilder now, his hands shaking. And the soldiers weren't letting up.

They were closing in.

Too many. Too organized.

Harlan reloaded.

And he knew—

They ain't winning this.

The only question was who makes it out alive.

CHAPTER 13: THE LAST STAND

Gunfire still snapped through the canyon, but it was slowing now, the sharp rhythm of it thinning out, breaking apart. It wasn't because the fight was ending. It was because there weren't many men left to shoot. The smell of blood and burnt powder sat thick in the air, choking up the space between the echoes of the last shots fired. The dust was heavy, swirling in the heat, coating every inch of exposed skin. The bodies lay where they fell—some sprawled in the dirt, some crumpled against the jagged rock, their blood soaking into the dry, cracked ground.

The gang was hemorrhaging men. Some dead. Some too gut-shot or crippled to keep fighting. Those still breathing dragged themselves toward cover, pressing hands against wounds, muttering half-formed prayers to gods who weren't listening. And yet, McKinnrick wasn't moving. He stood in the middle of it all, revolver still smoking in his grip, his face carved from stone. His eyes weren't on the dead, weren't on the men falling around him. They were locked on one thing.

The wagon.

Harlan saw it plain as day now—this fight was lost.

There weren't enough of them left to hold the ridge, let alone make a stand. The Army wasn't breaking. The law was closing in. They had to go. Harlan shoved forward, grabbing McKinnrick's arm, pulling hard enough to snap him out of whatever spell he'd fallen into. "We gotta go, McKinnrick. This ain't winnable."

He expected McKinnrick to curse, to bark an order, to start moving. But the man just turned his head slow, his expression something dangerous. Something hollow. His eyes weren't the eyes of a man thinking about survival. They were the eyes of a man thinking about gold.

McKinnrick let out a breath, slow, measured, and then his lips curled—not in a smile, not in amusement, but in something that sat just on the edge of madness. "That strongbox is still sittin' there, ain't it?"

The words made Harlan's stomach drop. He pulled back slightly, his grip still tight on McKinnrick's arm, but his fingers going slack.

"Jesus Christ, are you even hearin' me?" Harlan said, voice sharp. "We're done, McKinnrick. This is over."

McKinnrick's jaw twitched, his grip flexing on his revolver. His body was tense, like a coil ready to snap. He wasn't leaving. Wasn't retreating. He wasn't even considering it. He wouldn't walk away without what he came for. Didn't matter that half the gang was already dead. Didn't matter that the noose was already waiting for whoever lived through this. All that mattered was the goddamn gold. And Harlan suddenly realized—this was it. This was the moment. He had to decide. Stay and die with him. Or turn his back on McKinnrick before the bullets or the law made the choice for him.

Harlan heard it before he saw it. A distant thunder, low but growing—hoofbeats pounding against the hard-packed earth, fast and sharp, moving like they meant business. He turned his head toward the mouth of the canyon, wiping the sweat and dust from his brow with the back of his sleeve. A sick feeling curled in his gut.

Then he saw them.

Riders.

A line of dark shapes emerging from the haze of heat and dust, moving with a deliberate pace, rifles slung across saddles, pistols loose at their hips. Harlan squinted against the glare, taking in the lead figure. A broad-shouldered man, moving easy in his saddle, a shotgun resting across his lap like an afterthought. His face was shaded beneath the brim of a sweat-stained hat, but Harlan didn't need to see his eyes to know what he was.

Lawmen.

"Oh, hell," Harlan muttered, his stomach turning to lead.

McKinnrick saw them too, lifting his head from where he was staring at the strongbox, his gaze narrowing toward the approaching posse. The last flickers of greed on his face were gone now, replaced by something cold. Calculating.

Poe had stopped shooting long enough to follow Harlan's gaze. The moment he saw the riders, his grin vanished. "Shit."

Dixon, still half-slumped against the ridge, groaned through gritted teeth. "Ain't no way those bastards came here to take prisoners."

The gang was trapped. Soldiers to the front. Lawmen to the back. No way out except straight through. Harlan's mind raced, scanning the canyon for an opening, an escape route, anything—but there was nowhere to go. The pass was a choke point, a death box. The same thing that had made it the perfect spot for an ambush was now working against them. McKinnrick had planned to trap the payroll wagon here. Instead, he'd led them straight into their own goddamn grave.

The **lawmen reined up**, their horses lathered with sweat from the hard ride, flanks streaked white from the effort. They spread out in a loose formation, **deliberate, practiced**, rifles and shotguns braced across their saddles. They weren't in a hurry. **They knew they had the upper hand.**

The lead man, **broad-shouldered with a tin star pinned to his chest**, nudged his horse forward, stopping just out of easy gun range. **A shotgun rested in his grip, steady, ready.** His expression was **stone-flat, unreadable**, the kind of face that didn't give anything away unless it meant to.

He let his eyes move across the wreckage of the fight—the bodies sprawled in the dirt, **some dead, some moaning**, the blood soaking into the dry ground. The **wagon still stood**, battered but holding, soldiers crouched behind it, rifles ready. **McKinnrick's gang had nowhere left to run.**

Finally, the sheriff let his gaze settle on **McKinnrick**, and a slow smile curled at the edges of his mouth.

"You look like hell... Wells."

Harlan felt something shift in his gut.

Wells.

That was McKinnrick's old name. The one Cutter had mentioned. The name he'd used before they fled south, before he rebuilt himself as **a**

lawman, a bounty hunter, a man who still pretended he was on the right side of things.

And now it had caught up to him.

McKinnrick **didn't flinch**, but Harlan could see it—the tightening of his jaw, the way his hand hovered just near his gun belt. He was measuring the odds. And for the first time since Harlan had met him, it didn't look like McKinnrick liked his chances. Harlan felt his pulse pick up, the tension ratcheting tight as a noose. This wasn't a standoff. This wasn't a negotiation. This was a firing squad waiting to happen. And if Harlan didn't do something—anything—he was going down with them.

The gunfire had slowed to sporadic bursts, the kind of shots meant to keep McKinnrick's men pinned down. The sharp snap of a rifle, the occasional pistol crack, the distant groan of the dying filled the gaps in the silence.

Harlan's breath came short and tight, his body still braced for another volley, another rush of violence. But the lawmen weren't firing yet. They were waiting. Letting the dust settle. Letting the moment stretch.

And McKinnrick, in all his damn pride and arrogance, still hadn't moved.

Harlan turned his head, trying to take stock—who was still standing, who wasn't. His eyes flicked to the bodies strewn across the canyon floor. Dixon was still breathing, though not by much. Poe was muttering to himself, rolling his shoulder like he'd caught a graze.

Then Harlan saw him.

The soldier. The kid couldn't have been more than eighteen, nineteen tops. Just a boy. He was on his stomach, dragging himself toward a fallen rifle, fingers barely curling around the stock. His uniform was dark with blood, soaked through at the ribs, but he kept moving, his breath ragged and wet. He was dying. That much was certain. But he wasn't a threat. Not anymore. The law was still perched on the ridge, the posse waiting for McKinnrick to make his move.

That's when the shot rang out.

Loud. Sharp. Final.

Harlan froze mid-step.

Turned his head just in time to see McKinnrick lowering his revolver, the barrel still smoking. The soldier wasn't moving anymore. One clean hole through the side of his head, blood pooling fast in the dust. A single shot. No hesitation. No mercy.

The gunfight had been chaos.

Wild. Brutal. Unforgiving.

But this wasn't that.

This wasn't a battle. This was an execution.

Harlan's stomach went tight.

He'd seen McKinnrick do bad things. Ugly things.

He knew the man was ruthless. Knew he'd cross lines Harlan wouldn't.

But this?

This was different.

The kid had already lost.

He had nothing left.

But McKinnrick killed him anyway.

Harlan's fingers curled into fists at his sides.

McKinnrick must've felt his stare, because he turned, locking eyes with Harlan. His face was calm.

Unreadable. Like it didn't mean a damn thing. Like the kid had just been another body in the dirt. And Harlan felt something shift deep in his gut. He'd been walking the edge with McKinnrick for weeks now.

But this?

This was the moment he knew. He couldn't ride with this man anymore. Couldn't be part of this. And he sure as hell wasn't gonna die for him. The canyon smelled of blood, dust, and spent gunpowder. The echoes of gunfire still rang off the rock walls, but the fight itself had died down. What was left now was the slow kind of killing. The waiting. The final choices.

And McKinnrick was still standing there, not seeing the bodies, not seeing the law closing in.

Just the strongbox.

Harlan had seen men fall apart in battle before.

Men who'd started out loud and sure, but by the time the lead started flying and the bodies started dropping, they weren't so bold anymore.

And he was seeing it again now.

The gang was done.

There weren't enough of them left to fight, and the ones still breathing knew it.

The kid McKinnrick had just shot was still bleeding out in the dirt, his body twisted wrong, and something about that moment took the last bit of fight out of them. The men had been willing to kill. They'd been willing to steal, to burn, to take what they wanted.

But now?

Now, they weren't willing to die for it. Across the canyon, a man let out a slow breath and let his gun drop. It hit the dirt with a dull thud. The man—Briggs, one of the newer recruits—raised both hands high, his eyes flicking between McKinnrick and the sheriff's posse.

"I ain't dyin' for this, McKinnrick." His voice was steady, but there was fear in it. The kind that came when a man saw his own grave right in front of him. "Don't matter if we take the gold or not—we ain't gettin' out of here."

Nobody argued.

A second man—Rowley, one of Dixon's boys—started backing up, glancing toward the canyon's edge like he was thinking about making a run for it. Harlan almost opened his mouth to stop him. But it was too late. The shot came from the ridge. Rowley jerked, his body snapping forward like someone had yanked a rope around his chest. The sound of the gunshot came a second later.

A clean shot. Right through the back.

He collapsed in the dirt, twitched once, then went still.

Harlan's stomach twisted.

A soldier had done the shooting, probably one of the scouts still picking targets from the high ground. And just like that, every man still standing knew there was no running. Not unless you wanted to catch a bullet in the spine.

And McKinnrick?

McKinnrick didn't even turn his head.

Didn't flinch when the gun went off.

Didn't look when Rowley's body hit the dirt.

Maybe he saw it.

Maybe he didn't.

Maybe he just didn't care.

Because his eyes were still on one thing.

The strongbox.

Harlan stared at him, his breath coming slow and measured. McKinnrick had lost the fight. The gang was broken, bleeding out into the dirt. And Harlan knew, with every sharp instinct in his body, that if he stuck with him now, he was as good as dead.

This was the moment.

CHAPTER 14: MCKINNRICK'S FALL

The dust had started to settle. Not completely—not enough for things to feel over—but just enough that the last echoes of gunfire faded into the canyon walls, swallowed up by the silence that followed. The air was thick with the stink of powder and blood, the heat still pressing down like a weight. And in the middle of it all, McKinnrick stood tall, refusing to move. His revolver still sat firm in his grip, his knuckles white, but it didn't matter now. There was no one left to shoot. His men were either dead or on their knees. The soldiers were still standing, reloading, watching.

And the law? They had him dead to rights. The sheriff adjusted the shotgun in his hands. He was watching McKinnrick like a man watching a rattlesnake that hadn't decided whether it was dead yet.

He spat once into the dust, then said, loud enough for every man still breathing to hear him— "It's over, Wells. You put that iron down, maybe I don't gut-shoot you." His voice was calm. Measured.

But Harlan had spent enough time around killers to hear the edge underneath it. The sheriff wasn't making a deal. He was giving McKinnrick a chance to die with his boots on.

McKinnrick stood real still, real quiet. Then he laughed. It was a dry, broken sound, a cough more than anything, blood catching between his teeth. When he turned his head, Harlan saw the red smeared across his grin, like he was already bleeding out from the inside. He knew how this ended. And he didn't give a damn. Instead of dropping the revolver, instead of raising his hands, McKinnrick did something that made Harlan's gut tighten into a hard knot of dread.

He raised the gun.

Not at the sheriff.

Not at the soldiers.

At the strongbox.

That iron-plated thing, still sitting in the wrecked wagon, untouched, unopened, the thing he had killed for, the thing he had bled for. Harlan realized what was about to happen half a second too late. McKinnrick was gonna put a bullet in it. As if that would make up for the men who died trying to steal it. As if one shot, one last act of defiance, would turn this failure into something else. Something that mattered.

The shot never came. A rifle cracked. The bark of the gunshot was sharp and sudden, cutting through the heavy air like a blade. McKinnrick's body jerked, a violent snap backward, as the bullet tore through his ribs. For a second, he stayed on his feet, his mind trying to catch up to the fact that he was already dead. Then his knees buckled. The revolver slipped from his fingers, clattering onto the dirt. He staggered once, twice—

And then he fell.

Face-first, hitting the ground with a dull, lifeless thud.

The silence that followed was different from before. It wasn't the pause between gunfire, the tense breath before the next shot. This was final. A silence that meant it was over. The dust swirled around McKinnrick's body, already settling over him. Like the land didn't much care that he'd ever been there.

The gunfight was over, but the killing wasn't. The air was still thick with the smell of blood, powder, and hot dust, the canyon floor a mess of bodies—some moaning, some still, some never getting up again. The echoes of gunfire had faded, leaving only the low groans of the dying and the sharp, barked orders of the lawmen as they rounded up whoever was left.

But Harlan wasn't about to get hauled in. He saw Dixon on his knees, bleeding, hands laced behind his head as one of sherrif's men yanked his gun belt off. Briggs had surrendered too, sitting slumped against a rock, staring at nothing, the will to fight drained out of him. Across the way, Poe stood still as stone, his hands raised, staring down the barrels of three different rifles. His usual smirk was gone, and for the first time, Harlan saw something close to fear in the man's eyes.

They weren't shooting anymore. Now they were cleaning up. And Harlan knew what that meant. They weren't hauling these men back to Garrison for a fair trial. This was gonna end with a short rope and a long drop. For all of them.

He turned, already making his move, slipping between the boulders, angling toward the wrecked wagon. If he could just get to the edge of the canyon, find a horse, maybe he could—

The shot came from nowhere.

A sharp crack, too close, too sudden.

The bullet tore into his side. Harlan grunted, stumbling, catching himself against the hot stone with one hand. The pain flared deep and searing, a sharp burst of heat radiating through his ribs.

Not a kill shot.

But bad enough.

His breath hitched as he pressed a palm to the wound, feeling the wet, sticky heat of blood seeping fast. He swayed, his vision tunneling for half a second. The canyon spun around him, the world turning hazy at the edges.

No.

Not like this.

He forced his knees to lock, forced his boots to hold. He wasn't gonna die here in the dust with McKinnrick's corpse and the rest of the fools who followed him. He had seconds to decide. Stay put and bleed out. Get caught and hanged.

Or run.

Harlan gritted his teeth, wiped the blood from his palm onto his jeans, and took a breath so sharp it burned. There was only one choice. He had to ride. Harlan stumbled forward, one hand clamped tight to his side, his breath coming fast and ragged. The wound was bad—he could feel the warmth of his own blood seeping through his fingers, slick and hot, dripping into the dust. But he couldn't stop. Couldn't slow down.

Not with the law still standing, their guns still loaded, and the bodies of McKinnrick's men crumpled all around him. His boots slid in the dirt as he made his way toward the dead soldiers' horses, scanning the ones that had gone down, hoping—praying—one was still alive.

Then he saw it.

A dun-colored gelding, its flanks streaked with sweat, nostrils flaring wide, stamping its hooves against the ground. The saddle was still intact, the reins dragging through the dirt. A chance. A way out. Harlan moved fast, gritting his teeth through the pain, every step jarring the bullet wound in his side. The animal tossed its head as he reached for the reins, sensing the panic in his movements.

"Easy, boy," Harlan muttered through clenched teeth, tightening his grip. "We ain't got time for nerves."

The gelding snorted, shifting sideways, but it didn't bolt. That was all the permission Harlan needed. He hauled himself up into the saddle, every muscle screaming. His vision swam, dark spots creeping at the edges. His hand was still pressed hard to his ribs, trying to slow the bleeding, but the strength was draining from his fingers.

He could hear the law moving behind him, barking orders, the click of revolvers being cocked.

Then the shout—

"Stop him!"

A rifle cracked. The shot whistled past his head, hitting rock, sending sharp stone fragments slicing through the air. Harlan ducked low in the saddle, legs clamping tight around the horse's sides. No more time. No more chances. He kicked the gelding hard. The animal bolted forward, dirt exploding beneath its hooves, the sudden jolt sending another burst of pain through Harlan's ribs.

Didn't matter.

Didn't stop him.

He rode straight through the wreckage of the fight, past the blood-soaked dust, past the twisted, lifeless bodies of McKinnrick's men. And as he passed, his eyes flicked once, just once, toward the spot where McKinnrick had fallen.

Harlan didn't look back again. Didn't glance at the bodies, the dead men, the blood soaking into the dirt. He just rode.

Hard.

Fast.

As far away from Devil's Pass as the horse could carry him.

Harlan's breath came ragged and uneven, every inhale dragging fire through his ribs. The wound was bad, but not enough to stop him. Not enough to keep him here.

The desert stretched wide in front of him, an endless sea of dust and heat, the horizon blurred by the last lingering rays of sun. Behind him, Devil's Pass was falling into silence. The law had their prisoners. The dead had found their graves in the dirt.

And McKinnrick?

McKinnrick wasn't a name that mattered anymore.

His vision swam, the blood loss making everything feel distant, like he was barely inside his own skin. He could feel the sticky warmth trailing from his side, soaking into his shirt, but he didn't stop riding. Didn't slow. He just kept his grip tight on the reins and his eyes forward.

He wasn't gonna die here.

Not in a canyon littered with the bones of fools who thought they could take on the law and win. Not in the same dirt where McKinnrick had fallen, thinking he could cheat fate with a gun and a dream of stolen gold. Harlan had never been a man made for dying in one place. He had too much of the road in him, too much of the drift, too many miles waiting ahead.

He didn't know where he was going.

Didn't know what came next.

But he knew one thing.

He ain't ever gonna hear the name McKinnrick again.

And if he does?

He'll pretend he never knew him.

He pressed his heels into the horse's sides, riding harder, leaving the past behind him in the dust.

CHAPTER 15: BLEEDING AND RUNNING

Harlan rode hard, but his body was quitting on him. His hands felt loose and slick against the reins, the strength in his fingers leaking out with the blood seeping through his side. The pain was a hot, pulsing thing, burrowing deep between his ribs, carving its own path with every jolt of the horse beneath him.

He could taste copper and dust, could feel the way his breath hitched every time the wound throbbed too deep. The sun was low on the horizon, but the heat still clung to the land, making the air feel thick and dry in his throat. The desert stretched wide and empty ahead of him, no sign of pursuit— but he didn't trust it. Didn't trust that sheriff or his men wouldn't decide to chase him down, put a bullet in his back just for good measure.

Didn't trust that the soldiers wouldn't send a scout after him, track him like a wounded animal across the sand. Didn't trust anything except the horse beneath him and the fact that he was still breathing. And even that felt shaky. His mind drifted, flickering in and out of focus, like his body was on the verge of deciding whether to keep going or just let go.

McKinnrick's body, face-down in the dirt. The way the dust had already started settling over him, like the land had moved on before he even took his last breath. The gunfight in the canyon. The sharp bite of bullets tearing through air, the bodies hitting the ground one after another, the shouts, the screams. The kid soldier, crawling for his rifle—

before McKinnrick put him down. That one stuck the hardest.

The look on the kid's face. The desperation. He hadn't been reaching for a gun to kill. He had been reaching because he had nothing else left. And McKinnrick had ended him anyway. Harlan could still see it. Could still hear the gunshot, still see the blood blooming out into the dirt. And how close he had come to being the man who pulled the trigger.

He gritted his teeth and forced his mind back into the present. His grip tightened on the reins, fingers stiff and weak, but still holding. He wasn't gonna die out here. Not in the middle of nowhere, bleeding into his saddle like a man too stupid to know when he was finished.

Not like McKinnrick.

He had to keep going.

Had to stay upright.

Had to find a place to hole up, before the blood loss made the choice for him.

The horse snorted, tossing its head as Harlan nudged his heels into its sides, pushing it forward. He wasn't ready to die yet. And so long as he could keep moving, he wouldn't. The desert swallowed the last of the sun, the sky shifting to deep purples and burnt oranges, the land stretching endless in all directions. The heat of the day lingered in the dirt, radiating back up in slow, dying waves, but the cool of the night was creeping in now, settling into the cracks of the land like something alive. Harlan rode with half-lidded eyes, his body running on nothing but instinct, his fingers still curled tight around the reins, though he wasn't sure if he was even holding them anymore or if they were just there, tangled in his grip.

His head swayed with the horse's movements, the edges of his vision blurring, swimming in and out of darkness. He needed to stop. But stopping meant dying in the sand, and he wasn't ready for that yet. Then he saw it. A dark shape against the land, barely more than a shadow in the dimming light. At first, he thought it was just another rock outcrop, the kind that littered the desert, jagged and worn down by wind and time.

But as he rode closer, he saw the straight lines of it. The slumped angles. The way it caught just enough moonlight to show weathered wood instead of stone.

A shack. Old. Falling apart. But still standing. Harlan exhaled, slow and ragged, barely aware he'd been holding his breath. It wasn't much. Hell, it might not even have a damn roof. But it was shelter. And right now, that was enough. The gelding tossed its head, nostrils flaring, sensing Harlan's exhaustion, its own steps slowing as if to tell him they were both about done.

Harlan pulled the reins, guiding the horse toward the shack, his movements sluggish. The closer he got, the more he could see how bad of shape the place was in—the walls leaned inward, the wood split and gray from too many years in the sun. The door hung half off its hinges, shifting with the wind, creaking in protest. But it was still standing. And that meant it would have to do.

Sliding out of the saddle was harder than he expected. His boots hit the dirt heavy, and for a second, his knees nearly buckled. His vision went black at the edges, the desert tilting beneath him. He reached out, steadying himself against the saddle, sucking in a breath through clenched teeth. Too much blood lost. Too much time spent pushing forward when he should've stopped hours ago. The horse shifted under his touch, ears flicking back toward him, sensing his weakness. Harlan gave the gelding a tired pat on the neck, muttering under his breath, though he wasn't sure what he was even saying.

Maybe just trying to convince himself he wasn't about to collapse. Maybe just trying to stay awake.

The shack's door groaned as he pushed it open, dust and stale air rushing out to meet him. The place was as bad inside as it looked outside. A rusted-out stove sat in one corner, its pipe bent and broken, a pile of ashes long gone cold beneath it. A few shattered bottles littered the floor, catching slivers of moonlight. Cobwebs hung from the ceiling, the corners of the room thick with years of dust and dead insects.

Harlan let his gaze drift, scanning the dark, looking for anything that might make this place worth crawling into.

Then he saw it. A cot. Old, the canvas sagging, one leg propped up with a brick. But still there. Still something to lay on that wasn't the goddamn dirt. That was good enough. His legs felt like they weren't his own as he stumbled toward it. He dropped down onto the cot, hissing through his teeth as pain shot through his ribs, the wound pulling tight. Didn't matter. He was off his feet. Under some kind of roof. Still breathing. That was all that mattered. For now.

The silence in the shack felt too thick, too heavy, like the air itself had settled around him, pressing down with the weight of everything he'd left behind in Devil's Pass. Harlan let his head rest against the rough wood of the wall, his breath coming slow, uneven. He could feel the warm stickiness of blood against his ribs, the way it had seeped into his shirt, clinging to his skin like a second layer. He needed to clean it. Needed to see how bad it really was. With a slow, measured breath, he reached up and unbuckled his gun belt, setting it within arm's reach on the floor. Just in case. Then he worked his arms out of his coat, the movement sending a sharp spike of pain through his side. He sucked in a breath, gritting his teeth against the burn, then let the coat drop onto the cot beside him.

The shirt was worse.

The dried blood had sealed parts of the fabric to his skin, and the second he tried peeling it away, the wound beneath it screamed back at him.

"Shit." He exhaled slow, steadying himself.

No way around it. Had to get it over with. With one hard pull, he yanked the shirt open, the buttons popping loose, the dried blood tearing away from the wound like old scabs ripped raw. Pain flared bright and sharp, like something white-hot being dragged across his ribs. He clenched his jaw, his breath hissing through his teeth, but he didn't make a sound beyond that.

No point. Pain wasn't new. It just meant he was still breathing.

He looked down at the wound. It wasn't a clean shot through, but it wasn't deep enough to kill him, either. The bullet had grazed along his ribs, tearing a raw, bloody path, leaving the skin and muscle jagged, burning. Could've been worse. Hell, it should've been worse. He'd been lucky. Again.

But luck had a way of turning bad quick. He scanned the room, looking for anything useful. His eyes caught a dust-covered tin basin in the corner, sitting beneath the rusted-out stove. Might not be clean, but it'd hold water. That was enough. He reached for his canteen, popped the cap off, and poured what was left into the basin. The water sloshed, muddying with dust and old grime. Didn't matter. Better than nothing. He set his jaw, dipped his fingers in the cool water, and braced himself.

The second he touched the wound, the pain shot through him like fire, his whole body tensing on instinct. His hand clenched around the edge of the basin, knuckles white, but he didn't stop. Didn't slow down. He worked quick and rough, dragging the wet cloth across the wound, clearing away the caked blood and dust. His breath stayed tight, sharp, but he kept going, letting the pain settle into something steady, something manageable.

A part of him figured he'd earned it.

A reminder.

A punishment.

Something to keep him from forgetting what he'd almost become. Once the wound was clean enough, he tore a strip from his ruined shirt, wrapping it tight around his ribs. The pressure helped some, kept the worst of the bleeding under control. Didn't do a damn thing for the pain, though. But pain meant he was alive. And for now, that was enough.

He leaned back against the wall, letting himself breathe, letting the exhaustion weigh him down. His fingers brushed over his hands, over the stained skin, the dried blood still dark beneath his nails. Not all of it was his. And that thought sat heavier than anything else.

The silence inside the shack settled like dust after a long storm. No gunfire. No men barking orders. No law breathing down his neck. For the first time in days, he was alone. The fire in his ribs had dulled to a steady throb, something he could live with, something that would remind him he'd made it out. Made it through. But as Harlan sat there, his back pressed against the rough wooden wall, his breath slow and careful, the pain wasn't just in his side. It was in his chest. Heavy. Solid. A weight he couldn't shake. He had followed McKinnrick. Had ridden with him. Had let things slide—looked the other way when the gang bled a man for no reason, when they stole more than what they needed, when they hurt folks just because they could. And he'd kept moving forward, even when he knew it was wrong. Even when he felt it in his gut, that slow, creeping sickness that told him he was on the wrong side of the line.

And the worst part?

If McKinnrick had lived...

If that bullet hadn't cut him down...

Harlan might still be riding with him. That thought sat heavy and hard in his chest. McKinnrick had made choices. Easy choices. The kind of choices that men like him made when they stopped giving a damn about anything but themselves. And Harlan had been one step behind him the whole time. That was the kind of man McKinnrick had been. A man who didn't leave a road behind him—only bodies. And Harlan had almost been the same.

Harlan leaned his head back against the wall, staring at the cracked ceiling, watching the way the shadows stretched with the flickering light of the half-dead fire. His breath was steady but shallow. He was still bleeding. Still wanted. Still alone. But he wasn't McKinnrick. He wasn't that man. And now, he had to figure out what the hell came next.

CHAPTER 16: GHOSTS ON HIS TRAIL

Harlan rode through the dark, keeping off the trails, keeping low. The sky above him stretched wide and empty, a vast spread of stars flickering cold in the black. The moon sat low on the horizon, its light casting long shadows across the desert. He rode by it when he had to—just enough to see, never enough to be seen. The wound in his ribs still ached something fierce, pulling whenever he shifted in the saddle. The fever had broken two nights ago, but the weakness still clung to him, hiding in the corners of his bones, waiting.

Didn't matter.

Couldn't stop.

The land behind him might've been empty, but he never shook the feeling something was following. By dawn, he found himself riding along a dry wash, the cracked riverbed winding through the desert like an old scar.

It wasn't much, but it was cover. He let the horse walk slow, giving both of them a chance to breathe. He didn't know how many miles he'd put behind him since Devil's Pass, but it didn't feel like enough. Didn't feel like it ever would be. That uneasy feeling settled deeper when he spotted the dust cloud rising ahead. Harlan pulled back on the reins, narrowing his eyes against the early light. The cloud moved low and slow, curling up from beyond the next ridge. Riders.

He didn't know how many. Didn't know if they were just passing through. But he wasn't about to take that chance. He veered sharper off the wash, guiding his horse up the side of a rocky outcrop. Loose shale crunched beneath the hooves, but he kept the pace easy, careful. At the top, he slid from the saddle, wincing as his ribs pulled tight, then crouched low and waited.

The riders came into view. Five of them, maybe six, moving toward the watering hole below. Their horses moved with the ease of men who weren't running, but weren't in any hurry to be found either. Outlaws, maybe. Drifters like him.

Or worse.

Harlan shifted lower behind the rocks, keeping himself small, listening. Didn't take long before their voices carried. "Sheriff's got a bounty up," one of them said, his voice gravel-rough and low. Harlan's jaw tightened. He stayed still, listening. "Not just McKinnrick's men—him too. The drifter. The one that ran." Something in Harlan's gut went cold. "Sherrif wants 'im strung up."

"How much?"

"Enough. Dead or alive."

That was all Harlan needed to hear.

He slid back from the ridge slow and careful, his boots barely making a sound against the stone. Didn't wait to hear the rest. Didn't need to. The law had already made up its mind. They wanted his neck in a noose. And Harlan wasn't about to give it to them.

He climbed back into the saddle, pulling the reins tight.

Time to move. The town wasn't much. A handful of buildings huddled against the dust, sun-faded and leaning like they'd rather be anywhere else. A single road cut through the middle, rutted from wagon wheels, lined with horses hitched lazily outside storefronts. Harlan sat in the saddle just outside of town, taking it all in. It had the look of a place that didn't ask too many questions, where folks kept their heads down and did what needed doing. Good for passing through. Bad for staying.

Which suited him just fine.

He nudged his horse forward, keeping his pace slow, his presence small. His hat was pulled low over his face, his coat wrapped around him to hide the stiff way he carried himself. His ribs still burned, but pain didn't matter right now. Staying unnoticed did.

The general store sat squat and sturdy, the largest building in town aside from the saloon. A set of wooden steps led up to a porch, the planks groaning under Harlan's boots as he climbed them. A few horses were tied to the post outside, but the place was quiet.

A bell jangled dully as he pushed open the door, stepping inside.

The air was thick with dust and dry goods, the scent of old flour and leather mixing with the faint, stale musk of tobacco smoke. The light filtering through the windows was hazy, catching in the floating specks of dust.

Shelves lined the walls, stocked with the kind of necessities that kept men going—coffee, beans, bullets.

And behind the long wooden counter, a shopkeeper stood watching him.

Older. Broad in the shoulders but thick in the middle. His shirt stretched across a belly that had seen more good meals than bad. He had a face like a man who'd seen his share of trouble and didn't mind turning away from it if it kept business running smooth.

His eyes lingered on Harlan just a little too long.

"Need some food. Bandages. Whiskey," Harlan said, his voice slow, even.

The shopkeeper didn't move right away. He just squinted, chewing the inside of his cheek. "That so?" he said eventually, grabbing a bottle from behind the counter and setting it down with a thud. "Ain't seen you 'round here before."

Harlan held his gaze, kept his face unreadable. He was too tired to come up with anything clever, too sore to care. "Ain't been here before."

He reached into his pocket, pulled out a few silver coins, and set them down on the counter without a sound. The shopkeeper eyed them, then Harlan, then the coins again.

The silence stretched just a second too long.

Then—

"Name?"

Harlan didn't answer right away.

He didn't shift, didn't blink, just let the words settle between them like they hadn't been said at all.

He could feel it—that moment hanging in the air. Like the wrong move would set something loose, something he didn't want to deal with.

Then he exhaled slow, steady.

"Carter."

It wasn't much of a lie.

But it was enough.

The shopkeeper studied him for another second, then gave a grunt, sliding the coins into his apron pocket.

"Carter, huh." He reached under the counter, grabbing a small sack and stuffing it with supplies. "Don't figure you'll be staying long."

"Don't figure I will."

The shopkeeper nodded, handed over the sack. No more questions. Harlan took it, tipped his hat, and walked out. The moment he stepped outside, the air felt different. He had what he needed. A bottle of whiskey, a fresh canteen, some food to keep him moving. But something settled uneasy in his gut. Like someone was still watching. Like his name had left an echo in that store, and it wouldn't be long before someone asked about it. He adjusted his hat, kept his head low, and started toward his horse. It was time to go.

The saloon smelled of spilled whiskey, sweat, and bad decisions. The kind of place where men kept their backs to the wall and their hands close to their holsters. Harlan took a table in the farthest, darkest corner, his hat pulled low, his body angled where he could see the whole room without looking like he was trying to.

He wasn't here to drink. Not really. But a man sitting alone in a saloon without a drink in front of him? That caught attention. So he nursed a whiskey, letting the heat crawl down his throat slow, feeling it settle in his gut like an ember he wasn't sure would light or burn out.

And he listened. The talk was quiet, but it carried. Whispers bleeding through the noise. A few men at the bar, a couple at the tables, talking about things that weren't meant for every ear.

"Sheriff ain't done."

Harlan's fingers tightened around his glass.

"He's pickin' off what's left of McKinnrick's boys."

The words came low and steady, but Harlan heard every one of them like they were being spoken straight to him. A man at the bar, grizzled and dust-covered, shook his head as he sipped his beer.

"Saw Poe hangin' from a tree outside Clearwater."

Another man grunted, muttering into his drink.

Harlan felt something cold settle in his chest..

One of the younger men, a wiry thing with a nervous edge to his voice, leaned in. "Heard there's still one or two hidin' in the hills, but it won't last."

The older man gave a slow nod, tossing back another gulp of beer. "Nope. Ain't lastin' at all."

A pause. Then a chuckle. "Reckon there's only one left worth lookin' for."

Harlan didn't move. Didn't blink. Just stared into his glass, watching the whiskey turn lazy in the lamplight. They were hunting McKinnrick's men. One by one. And if they found him? Harlan let out a slow breath, pushing his glass aside.

Time to move.

He stood, his joints stiff from too many miles, too many nights sleeping in the dirt. He didn't rush. Didn't give off the look of a man leaving in a hurry. Hurrying got you noticed.

And right now, Harlan didn't want to be noticed.

He slid through the tables, past the men talking about his own damn death warrant, and stepped out into the night. The air outside was cooler than it should've been. A sharp wind cutting through the heat left behind by the sun. But something felt wrong. The town was quiet, save for the rattle of a sign in the breeze, the distant stomp of a horse shifting in its tether.

And then—

A scent carried on the wind.

Gun oil. Sweat. Trouble. Harlan didn't turn around fast. Didn't snap his head like a man who'd just realized he was being watched. He just listened. The creak of leather. The soft scrape of boots shifting in the dirt. Someone was watching him. Hunting him.

And he had to decide fast—

Run. Or fight.

Run.

CHAPTER 17: NO PLACE LEFT TO RUN

The desert stretched wide and empty beneath the low-hanging moon, silver light casting long shadows across the earth. Harlan rode slow, his hat low over his brow, the reins loose in his grip. The only sound was the steady clop of hooves against hard-packed dirt and the occasional whisper of wind dragging through dry brush.

He'd lost track of how many nights he'd been riding, how many miles he'd put between himself and Devil's Pass, between himself and McKinnrick's corpse, between himself and the law. But distance didn't change the truth.

He was a wanted man. And running wasn't gonna fix that. His ribs still ached from the wound he'd taken back in the canyon, a sharp pull every time the horse shifted beneath him. The pain had dulled, but it never let him forget.

Same as everything else. The faces of the dead haunted his mind. McKinnrick, lying in the dust, his fingers twitching like he was trying to grab hold of something that wasn't there. Dixon, shot down like a dog trying to flee across the border. Cutter, swinging from a tree outside Clearwater.

Harlan had thought leaving that life behind meant he could put it in the ground with the men who'd lived it. But the past wasn't a thing you could bury. Especially not when the law was digging it right back up.

The realization had been creeping in slow, curling at the edges of his mind ever since he'd heard his name spoken over a campfire, whispered in a saloon. Sheriff Grady put a bounty on him. Not just the men who had followed McKinnrick. Him, too. Didn't matter that he'd only got tangled up in this mess because some drunken gambler had tried to shoot him and he'd got in first.

Harlan let out a slow breath, staring out at the endless stretch of land ahead. The old him would've kept running. Would've ridden farther, changed trails, kept ahead of the hunters until his luck ran out.

But luck always ran out. Didn't matter how far he rode, a name on a bounty poster didn't disappear. Not unless he found a way to clear it. The problem was, he didn't have the first damn idea how. He rode on, his thoughts heavy, his body sore. The land was dark ahead, a road without an end, without a destination. All he knew was one thing—He needed to disappear.

The town sat low and sprawling against the desert, the kind of place that had outgrown itself just enough to think it was something more than a stop between nowhere and somewhere worse. Bigger than the settlements he'd passed through the last few weeks. Enough buildings to matter, enough people to keep moving. Bustling, but not crowded. It had a proper main street, lined with storefronts and a handful of saloons, dust kicking up under the wheels of wagons moving slow through the afternoon heat.

Harlan reined his horse in at the edge of town, sitting back in the saddle, taking it in. He wasn't the only newcomer—a handful of riders moved through, passing through on their own business, wagons loaded with trade, a few drifters loitering outside the saloons. It was the kind of town where people noticed a stranger, but they didn't care enough to ask questions if he kept to himself. That was what he needed. He nudged his horse forward, letting the town swallow him up.

He rode slow down the main street, keeping his eyes open, his head down just enough not to invite too much attention. He took in the details—a barber's shop, a tailor's, a general store, a gunsmith. The important things. He passed a group of men unloading a wagon, one of them pausing just long enough to glance at him, then turn back to his work. No one recognized him. Not yet. Still, he felt the weight of his own name chasing him.

Wanted. Dead or alive.

The bounty was out there, his name inked onto posters, hanging in places just like this. Didn't matter that he wasn't the worst of them. Didn't matter that he'd run before the blood dried in Devil's Pass. The law wasn't looking for the truth. They were looking for bodies.

His mother once told him the best place to hide was in plain sight. She'd been talking about hiding a piece of stolen silverware from his uncle when he was a boy, but the lesson stuck. And right now, he needed to hide. He passed a hitching post outside the barber's shop and pulled his horse to a stop, swinging down from the saddle with a slow, practiced motion. The stiffness in his ribs was still there, the dull ache of healing flesh, but he ignored it. Had to.

He tied the horse off, adjusted his hat, and stepped inside. The door swung shut behind him, cutting off the noise of the street. The air inside was thick with the scent of pipe smoke and shaving soap, the low murmur of conversation barely filling the space. A handful of men sat waiting, boots tapping idly against the wooden floor. The barber, an older man with a belly that spoke to better years, glanced up from where he was stropping a razor.

Harlan met his eye.

Harlan pulled off his hat, ran a hand through his hair, feeling the grease and grit in it. Then he let himself settle into the chair. "Make me look like someone else."

The barber nodded toward the chair. "Take a seat."

Harlan did.

The blade scraped slow across his jaw, peeling away the man he'd been for the past few months. The barber worked without hurry, without questions, the quiet snick of the razor filling the space between them. Each pass of the blade revealed something sharper, cleaner, like he was cutting Harlan down to the bone.

By the time it was done, Harlan barely recognized himself in the mirror.

His face was thinner than he remembered, the angles harder. The eyes staring back at him looked older, even if the rest of him was clean.

The barber dusted him off, gave a satisfied grunt. "That'll do you."

Harlan nodded, dropped another silver coin on the counter. Didn't say thank you. Didn't need to.

Then he walked out the door and into his next life. The tailor's shop was a small, narrow building crammed with too much fabric and not enough light. The air smelled of starch, mothballs, and old leather. Bolts of cloth leaned against the walls, a few jackets and shirts hanging from pegs behind the counter. An old man with round glasses perched on his nose looked up as Harlan stepped inside, taking in the fresh shave, the worn clothes, the careful way Harlan moved.

"Looking for something particular?" the tailor asked.

Harlan let his fingers trail over the edge of a black coat hanging nearby, the fabric smooth beneath his fingertips. It was well-cut but not flashy, the kind of thing a man could wear into a saloon without standing out too much, but fine enough to pass for someone with a bit of money. "Something that don't make me look like I've been sleeping in the dirt."

The tailor chuckled, his round glasses slipping lower on his nose as he sized Harlan up. "Got plenty that fits that bill." Then his expression shifted, a wary edge creeping in. His fingers tapped against the wooden counter. "You got coin, mister?"

Harlan let the question sit in the air for a second. He'd seen that look before—a shopkeeper measuring a man, deciding if he was worth the trouble, if he'd walk out owing money or if he could pay up front. He reached into his coat, pulled out a small leather pouch, and tossed it onto the counter with a quiet clink of silver.

The tailor raised an eyebrow but said nothing.

Yeah, he had money. More than he ought to. More than a man like him should be carrying. McKinnrick's money.

Harlan ignored the weight of that thought, gesturing toward the coat again. "That one'll do."

The crisp white shirt underneath felt foreign against his skin after so long in sweat-stiffened cotton, the vest snug but comfortable. The trousers were clean, pressed, not fancy but well-made, the kind a man wore when he wanted to look like money without carrying a dime of it. When he stepped in front of the mirror, he didn't look like the man who'd walked in.

The rough-edged drifter, the outlaw riding on borrowed time, was gone. In his place stood a gambling man, a sharp-dressed figure who could walk into any saloon and disappear into the background. He might've been a rancher come into money. A man down on his luck, looking for the next big win. Anything but what he really was.

Harlan paid in full, silver coins landing on the counter in a dull clink. The money came from McKinnrick, stolen and stained with blood, but right now it was keeping him alive. As he stepped back onto the street, adjusting his coat, the town didn't look at him the same way.

He didn't look like a wanted man. Didn't look like an outlaw. But as he turned the silver dollar in his palm, something nagged at him. He didn't know if he felt different.

Not yet.

The streets were turning soft with twilight, lanterns flickering to life along the storefronts, their yellow glow pushing weak against the deepening blue of the sky. The town had settled into its evening rhythm—the laborers coming in from the fields and cattle yards, the drifters and card sharps stretching into the night. Harlan pulled his coat snug over his shoulders, adjusting the cuffs of his crisp new shirt. He felt the weight of the fabric, the smoothness of the vest beneath his fingers. He'd worn finer clothes before, years ago, in another life.

But this wasn't about looking good.

This was about disappearing.

The saloon stood ahead, double doors yawning open, leaking light and laughter onto the street. The sound of a piano drifted out, slightly out of tune but still lively, keeping pace with the murmur of conversation inside.

Harlan walked in slow.

The air inside was thick with whiskey, sweat, and tobacco smoke, the kind of mix that had settled deep into the floorboards, making the place feel older than it was.

He didn't move fast, didn't draw attention. Just let his boots find the rhythm of the place, the easy, unhurried pace of a man looking to pass the time.

No one spared him more than a glance.

A group of men hunched over a poker table, cards in their hands, stacks of coins between them. Gamblers, but not professionals. A few ranch hands playing loose with their wages, a drifter trying his luck, the dealer watching them all with the blank patience of a man who'd seen it all before.

A pair of working girls leaned against the far end of the bar, watching the doorway the way cats watched a mouse hole—waiting for the next man with coin to walk through.

The bartender, a heavyset man with a gut that stretched his apron tight, was cleaning a glass with slow, methodical movements. He looked up as Harlan approached, eyes flicking over him quick, assessing.

But there was no recognition. No hesitation.

No one waiting in the corner with a bounty poster in their lap.

No lawman watching him from the shadows.

For the first time in weeks, no one was looking for him.

Harlan slid onto a stool, the wood creaking softly under his weight. He let his hands rest on the counter, the new fabric of his sleeves strange against his wrists.

"Whiskey," he said.

The bartender nodded, turned, and poured without a word. The bottle clinked against the glass, a small splash rolling over the lip before settling.

Harlan lifted it slow, taking one careful sip, feeling the burn coil low in his stomach. Then he let his gaze shift, catching his own reflection in the mirror behind the bar. The man staring back at him wasn't the same one who had walked into town. No dust. No blood. No trail-worn drifter with eyes that looked too long at every doorway, waiting for trouble to come through it.

Instead, a clean-shaven man sat there in the low lamplight, his black coat draped easy over his shoulders, his vest smooth, his collar crisp.

A gambler. A traveler. A man who belonged.

Harlan watched that man for a long moment.

Then he tossed back the rest of the whiskey, let it burn all the way down, and set the glass aside.

Harlan sat at the bar, a freshly poured whiskey turning lazy in the glass, the lamplight catching in the amber depths. He turned it slow, watching it swirl, his mind working through the problem in front of him.

Carter wouldn't do.

That name belonged to a man who smelled of sweat and dust, a man who walked into towns with his hat pulled low and his collar turned up to keep his face in shadow. Carter was a man looking for a place to disappear.

But Harlan wasn't disappearing anymore.

Not yet, anyway.

He lifted the whiskey, took a slow sip, letting it burn low and warm in his chest. He needed a name that fit the man he looked like now. The man in the mirror behind the bar—clean-shaven, dressed sharp, someone who could sit at a poker table and play with men who had real money. A man who knew how to talk, how to bluff, how to slip through life without raising a single eyebrow.

But what name fit a man like that?

His eyes flicked up, scanning the bottles lining the shelves behind the bar. Rows of dark glass, their labels worn with time, familiar brands from the frontier. Names of men long dead, names of distillers and ranchers, names that had no history to him.

And then, he saw it.

McCoy.

The bottle sat among the rest, the lettering faded but clear enough.

Harlan felt the corner of his mouth pull into the smallest of smiles.

McCoy.

It felt right. It had weight to it, but not too much. It wasn't too clean, too noble—but it wasn't stained either. It was the kind of name a man could carry into a saloon, stake a few hands at a poker table, and walk out richer than he walked in. He'd keep his first name, Wesley was common enough.

McCoy was the kind of man who never had to run.

He lifted his glass again, took another slow sip.

Yeah.

Wesley McCoy would do just fine.

The disguise worked.

For now.

The night stretched quiet and cool, the heat of the day fading into the desert beyond the edge of town. Harlan walked slow, his boots scuffing against the hard-packed dirt, the weight of the fresh clothes settling against him like a second skin. The saloon doors swung shut behind him, muffling the laughter, the tinny sound of the out-of-tune piano, the low murmur of men chasing luck.

He cut through the alley behind the saloon, moving like a shadow between the dim pools of lantern light spilling from the back windows. The scent of old whiskey, piss, and kitchen scraps hung in the air, the kind of place most men hurried past without looking.

That was when he heard it.

A rustle. A soft scrape of movement.

Harlan slowed, instinct sharpening.

Then he saw him.

A kid—thin, dirty, crouched near a barrel, digging through scraps like a stray dog too hungry to wait for the daylight.

The boy had hollow cheeks, wide eyes, and quick hands—like he'd spent too much of his life learning how to grab and run. His clothes were nothing but patches and dirt, hanging loose over sharp bones.

He hadn't noticed Harlan yet, too focused on picking through what little had been left behind. A half-eaten piece of bread. A scrap of salted meat that had already started to curl.

Harlan exhaled slow.

He recognized that kind of hunger.

Had known it himself, once.

The kid must've felt the weight of Harlan's stare, because he froze, shoulders going stiff, hands tightening around the crust of bread like it might disappear if he let go.

Then, quick as a coyote, he spun, eyes darting toward Harlan, his body already braced to run.

Harlan raised a hand, palm out.

"Easy," he said. "Ain't got a mind to hurt you."

The kid didn't relax. Didn't move. Just watched him.

Harlan sighed, rolling his shoulders, letting the tension settle.

He reached into his pocket, fingers brushing against the silver coins he'd used to buy himself a new name.

Then he found it.

A single silver dollar, worn at the edges, catching a bit of moonlight as he pulled it free.

Harlan rolled it between his fingers, feeling the weight of it. Then, with a flick of his thumb, he sent it through the air.

The kid's hands were fast.

Snatched it right out of the air before it hit the dirt.

His eyes flicked between the coin and Harlan, suspicious. Confused.

Harlan just gave a small nod.

"That's yours now."

For a second, the kid didn't move, didn't speak, just held the coin like he was waiting for Harlan to take it back. Then, without a word, he turned and vanished into the dark, disappearing down the alley like smoke. Harlan stood there a moment, watching where he'd gone. The town was quiet. The wind stirred dust in the streets, ruffling the hem of his coat. The saloon still hummed behind him, full of men chasing luck, throwing down silver dollars they wouldn't remember come morning.

But Harlan would remember that one.

Not because of what it was.

Because of what it wasn't.

McKinnrick wouldn't have given that kid a damn thing. And for all the lines Harlan had blurred, for all the miles he'd ridden too close to the wrong kind of men, he wasn't that.

Not yet.

He tipped his hat lower, stepping out of the alley and toward his horse. The road stretched ahead, empty, waiting. His name was still out there. His past still hunted him. But at least tonight, he knew which direction he was heading.

EPILOGUE: A MAN CALLED MCCOY

The morning was crisp, the air carrying the sharp scent of sage and dust as Wesley McCoy nudged his new horse forward, the animal moving smooth and easy beneath him. It was a fine horse—better than the one he rode in on, sturdier, younger, with the kind of muscle that could take him far and fast. He'd traded up before leaving town, dropping a few of the last silver coins from McKinnrick's cursed stash into the hands of a horse trader who didn't ask too many questions.

McCoy adjusted his freshly filled saddlebags, feeling their weight against his back. Provisions, a little extra ammunition, and just enough whiskey to remind him he was still alive. He had what he needed. Nothing more. He was used to traveling light.

The town was waking up behind him. A few early risers moving about, the general store owner sweeping his front step, a pair of ranch hands crossing the street, laughing about something that didn't concern McCoy. No one gave him a second look.

That was the best part of a new name.

It didn't carry baggage yet.

Didn't have a bounty attached to it.

Didn't have blood on it.

Not yet, anyway.

The road stretched out ahead, long and empty, rolling toward the horizon like a slow-moving river of dust.

McCoy's Last Bet

McCoy let out a slow breath, tipping the brim of his new hat lower over his eyes.

He wasn't running anymore. He wasn't exactly settled either. A man like him never really was. But for the first time in a while, he wasn't looking over his shoulder, expecting the past to come up behind him. That past, the one belonging to a man named Nash, was dead.

McKinnrick was dead.

His old life, his old name—gone with them.

McCoy rolled a cigarette between his fingers, watching the dust swirl beneath his horse's hooves as they walked on. He didn't know exactly where he was headed. There were always towns needing a man good with a gun and bad at staying in one place. Always another job waiting for a man who knew how to read a card, call a bluff, and draw faster than the next fool with an itchy trigger finger.

Maybe he'd find himself at a poker table before sundown, buying in under a name no one knew. Maybe he'd ride into the next town and hear something that made him linger.

Or maybe trouble would find him first.

It usually did.

McCoy took one last look at the town shrinking behind him.

Then he put his cigarette between his lips, struck a match, and let the flame catch as he rode toward whatever came next. Because the thing about running from your past is, sooner or later, you run straight into your future. And McCoy had a feeling his future was waiting just over the next rise.

THE END

Please don't close the book just yet!

I'd like to thank you for reading, your time has been much appreciated, and I am heartened that you reached the end. This has been a work of love to bring back to life the tales left so many years ago by my grandfather's father in his journals. Stories of the old west, of times long forgotten and from people telling them as recent events. It has been a humbling experience to record these events and bring them back to life nearly 150 years later.

If you could spare a few moments to leave this ol' writer a review, and in doing so you'll be leaving one for the writer of the original journals, Declan Kelly, and those whose lives you've read about.

Next in the Series – McCoy's Final Hand

Made in the USA
Monee, IL
24 May 2025

18098890R00121